THE MADDY SAGA

BOOK THREE

PONYGIRL CHAMPION

BY

PAUL BLADES

Cover Art by Agnes Knox
agnesknox@simonas.se
agnes.knox@gmail.com

Dark Visions Publications
darkvisionspub@gmail.com

Previously published:

Vol. I   Maddy becomes a Ponygirl
Vol. II   The Training of a Ponygirl

Watch for publication of the other books in the Maddy Saga:

Vol. IV   Ponygirl Summer
Vol. V.   Ponygirl Love
Vol. VI   Ponygirl Season
Vol. VII   Ponygirl Gambit
Vol. VIII   Ponygirl Pleasures
Vol. IX   Ponygirl Peril
Vol. X   Ponygirl's Choice

Other books by Paul Blades:

Klitzman's Isle
Klitzman's Empire
Klitzman's Paradise
Klitzman's Pawn Part One
Klitzman's Pawn Part Two
The Taking of Cheryl Part One
The Taking of Cheryl Part Two: Slaver's Bait
Comfort Girl No. 4
Sacrifice to the Emerald God
The Blue Cantina: Anna's Surrender

CHAPTER ONE
A GIRL IS TRANSFORMED

"Jake, where the fuck is Maureen?" Irving screamed into the telephone, exasperated. "You told me that you would find out and let me know. It's been weeks and weeks. I want to know now!"

Jake Barnes was a fixer, an enforcer, a hard man of many talents and few scruples. He had been retained, together with his crew, by New York multi-millionaire Michael Burnham to find and rescue his niece, Madeline, who had been kidnapped one night on her way home from night classes at her local community college about 40 minutes northwest of Knoxville, Tennessee. They had traced Maddy, as she was called, to a farmhouse in Georgia where she was apparently held for some period of time before being shipped out to a slaving outfit located in northern New Jersey, close to the airports and the docks. Jake, with the help of Irving and other crew members had raided the slaver's headquarters only to find that Maddy had been shipped off to a small former Soviet Republic called Kalikastan to be turned into a ponygirl. There the trail had gone cold.

The problem was that when they raided the farmhouse in Georgia, they had found Maureen imprisoned in the kidnappers' underground dungeon. Jake, with a heart as cold as witch's tit, wanted to leave her there. Irving, the tech wizard, who sometimes served as the conscience of the group, would have none of it. He demanded that Maureen be rescued and saved from a cruel death of either starvation or thirst. Jake had called Burnham, whose operation it really was and who ultimately called the shots. A compromise was worked out. Burnham didn't want Maureen's recovery to jeopardize the mission to save Maddy. The reappearance of a kidnapping victim would attract press and cops. So it was agreed that Maureen would be shipped off to a private hospital of some kind where she would be kept comfortable, but incommunicado. Burnham, though, had other ideas. He hired some guys to get rid of what he saw as a problem. How could he know that Irving would be such a pain in the ass? Was he in love with her or something?

Anyway, there was no way that Burnham could tell Irving that Maureen had been 'taken care of' in an entirely different way than agreed upon. Burnham had done some checking and found out that she had been shipped off to Mexican slavers and was probably by now working on her back in some Mexican whorehouse. So, he kept stalling Jake, who kept stalling Irving.

"Listen, Irving, if I knew, I'd tell you," Jake responded, a little put out that his tech guy was hung up on a piece of ass. "Burnham's not telling me. He says it's a 'security' issue, 'need to know only'. Hopefully, we'll find Maddy soon and that will be the end of it."

"Listen, Jake, if anything has happened to Maureen, I'll be very, very pissed." Irving rang off.

Jake, in turn, was pissed at Burnham. Not only did he take umbrage at the suggestion that any of his guys couldn't be trusted, but he might need Irving. If Irving was pissed, or if something happened to Maureen that wasn't kosher, there would be hell to pay.

* * * * * * * * * * *

At the moment of Irving's telephone conversation with Jake, Maureen sat in the reception room of a Mexican whorehouse known as El Papaya, literally the succulent fruit, but also used as a colloquial expression for the fruit between a woman's thighs. She really didn't mind being a whore. It was much better than the dungeon that she thought she was going to spend the rest of her life in when she had been captured by that evil man and woman back in the States. Anywhere was better than that. She liked Irving. She had trusted Irving. But when the ambulance they had called to take her away had pulled out on the highway, they had given her an injection. Next thing she knew, she was locked in a tiny cage somewhere in Mexico. A few weeks later, she was here in this city that the other girls called Tuxtepec, wherever that was.

The Mexican city of Tuxtepec lies in the southern part of the State of Vera Cruz, at the eastern foothills of the Sierra Madre de Sur Mountains. Through it passes the wealth wrested from the mountains that lay to its west and north. Gold, silver and copper are the principal minerals mined there. Cotton is the mainstay of the many vast plantations to the south and east. Three times a year, a person flying over the broad plain would see a vast carpet of white laid out below.

The people of the area are generally poor. There are no unions in the Sierra Madres, nor labor organizers amidst the plantations. But there is vast wealth, concentrated in the hands of the so called 'Noble One Hundred', El Cientes Nobles. These are the hundred or so families that control the wealth of Tuxtepec and all of the area within two hundred miles. It had been that way for centuries, and all of the families claim heritage, some, of course, spuriously, going back to the influx of Spanish conquistadores that accompanied Cortez's conquest of the Aztec Empire.

The Cientes Nobles have governed the city of Tuxtepec through a kind of consensus since the time of Emperor Maximillan in the 1860's. Previously, factions had warred among themselves for control of the region. But they had banded together to support the overthrow of the French puppet and had lived in relative harmony ever since.

The city itself has retained most of its old world charms. Business is conducted mostly by handshake, and foreign capital and influences have been kept out. Since the plantations and mines are run mostly by the middle class overseers imported from central Mexico, the heads of family of the Cientes Nobles and their sons and their sons, and cousins and nephews and uncles, and all their friends, spend much of their time at leisure.

In the southern part of the city, three blocks off of Cinque de Mayo Boulevard, you can still find the gracious mansions that have housed the hordes of courtesans whose thighs and mouths have serviced what is jocularly referred to as el ciento nabos, or, the hundred cocks, for three hundred years. This upper class red light district covers about ten square blocks of the city. It is said that you can buy anything there.

Notorious among the many, refined houses of delight are the mansions that lie along the river on the western edge of the district. These houses cater to, let us say, the more esoteric of male demands. No one but the owners and operators of these specialized facilities know where the girls come from that suffer the many outrages freely visited on their bodies. For two centuries these mansions found their stock in trade in the various bandit raids that permeated the lands to the north. The beautiful wives and daughters of peones, bankers, farmers and governmental bureaucrats, and sometimes nobility, would find themselves tied to a mule and traveling deep into the Sierra Madres where bags of Tuxtepec gold was waiting to be exchanged for them. It did not take long to teach these women their new trade. And their light brown skin served as wonderful palettes for the long red welts left by a lash, or the deep purple wounds left by the riding crop.

In the last fifty years, these tawny whores have found themselves working side by side with the occasional disappeared Norte Americano or European tourist. In the last twenty, since the fall of the Soviet Union, a steady stream of Eastern European women have found their way here. Cries and screams in a literal polyglot of languages now fill the ancient rooms and halls. There is still the occasional Mayan beauty found here and there. But most of the 'workers' are undocumented, indentured women from the impoverished republics of the former Soviet Union and its faded empire.

This day, no one had selected Maureen for any afternoon delight. The other, pretty girls were gone. Maureen was, to be kind, plain in her features. She didn't mind fucking at all, in fact, she kind of liked it. But she was unfortunate to be what is known as a 'full figured girl', tall, with a heavy bone structure, prone to excess flesh. So she sat in the reception area alone, except for the bartender, waiting and hoping for a customer.

Upstairs, Esmeralda Jaoquim sat on her favorite easy chair in her private boudoir on the second floor. Her legs were spread and her loose cotton skirt was pulled to her waist. A blond head was between her thighs. It belonged to a former citizen of the former Workers' State. She was servicing her mistress.

Esmeralda was the handsome, fortyish madam and operating partner of this special house. She sat there dreamily as the well trained tongue of the Russian girl lapped at her loins. The girl was taking her time, as instructed. Madam needed this break from all the worries and cares of her day. Was Señor Gesalmo pleased? Did the Mayor's party have enough whores? Did she pay too much for the Canadian girls the day before?

She sighed as the Russian girl's tongue plunged deeply into her hole, licked the roof of her cunt, tickling it with its tip. She could sit there all day. Her body felt all alive, like a low voltage of electricity was flowing through her skin. The Russian's tongue was deliciously long and dexterous. Esmeralda looked down at the blond headed whore. Her wrists were tied behind her back and she was naked. She had beautiful, almost chalk white skin. Her hips were slender, her thighs graceful. The madam recalled her round and plump breasts, her areolas wide and deep maroon. It was too bad really. She was a terrific whore. But the resolution of difficult problems was her job and the partners expected her to keep all the important people happy.

Señor Monteñez was coming this afternoon to collect this little child of the tundra. He had a ranch up in the hills and every spring he came down to claim a few of her whores for the use of him and his vaqueros. They weren't worth much when they came back in the fall.

In fact, Monteñez was expected any moment. If she was going to get off, she better do it quickly.

The madam tapped the Russian girl's head lightly and ordered, "Aprisa! Rápidamente!" The girl's tongue and lips began working faster. She had kept the madam on a low burn for about half an hour. She seized her mistress's clit with the edge of her teeth and bit down softly. Esmeralda stiffened as the teasing pain created a wave of pleasure that flowed through her. The girl began lapping at the stiff bud. Her insistent tongue drove the madam's lusts higher and higher. Esmeralda gripped the arms of her easy chair and leaned her head back. As her release came, a throbbing, pounding convulsion of her whole body, she moaned and closed her eyes. "Oh, this whore is good!" she thought as her pussy sent her jolt after jolt of pleasure. "It's too bad she has to go."

When her contractions resolved, Esmeralda pulled on the blond hair that was still nestled between her thighs.

The pretty face of a nineteen year old Russian girl emerged. She had teardrop eyes and a small, pert nose. Her lips were thin, but her mouth was wide. She had a little rounded chin. Her eyes were cobalt blue. A beauty.

The deep blue eyes looked up at her mistress expectantly. She had learned to obey her mistress without question over the four weeks that she had been there. Days and nights of confinement plus a dance or two with the lash had persuaded her that obedience was the road to, if not happiness, at least a modicum of security from pain.

"Thank you, Raissa," Esmeralda told her. "Now please go stand in the corner there until I need you." The madam pointed to the far corner of the room. It was a spacious room, with several settees, a long, red, fluffy couch, side tables and lamps. The walls were also red, a deep, blood red, almost matching the torrid areolas of the Russian sex slave. The girl scurried to the corner and assumed a standing position, her legs closed, facing the joinder of the two walls.

The phone rang on the table next to Madam. "Yes," she answered. "He's done? How many?.....Three? And the other makes four!....Okay, send him up."

Four! Where did he think the girls came from, that they grew on trees? It has always been three. This required a telephone call to the senior partner.

Esmeralda walked over to her desk and picked up a cell phone. She dialed an international number. It rang three times. "Esmeralda," she said. A deep, laconic voice answered. "Yes?"

"The man from the mountains wants four oysters with his dinner."

"Four?" the deep voiced man repeated.

"Yes. Four."

"Well, give him what he wants; it's been a good year. I'll talk to him. Next year only three for sure."

"As you say," Esmeralda answered and hung up.

Just as she did there was a polite knock on her door. "Come," she said.

A tall, heavyset man entered. He had three days growth of beard and was wearing stiff denim trousers. His shirt was a deep orange, cotton work shirt. He had heavy, hand tooled, black leather boots. There were silver caps on the toes.

"Aya!" he said to her as he strode into the room. He covered the ten feet in two steps.

"Aya to you," Esmeralda returned to him.

"They've told you."

"Yes, four this year."

"My operations have expanded, I have more men. I need four," he explained.

"For now, it's settled," Esmeralda answered.

Monteñez ran a large cattle ranch. It was forty miles to the nearest village with a taverna. He didn't like the boys riding there each chance they got. And the nearest whorehouse was at least seventy miles. So he tried to give them all the amenities right where they worked. Of course two whores with fifty five to sixty men could get quite busy. And the third one was for him. His carnal demands were quite insatiable and he was a little rough with them. Last year he turned the girl over to the vaqueros before August. She was pretty much spent, but she still had three holes and was warm and breathing. He had to buy a girl on the open market. He was a cheap bastard. So this year he wanted four.

He usually wintered in the city, where whores could be found quite cheaply. Many of them had no families. Mezstizos, mostly. No one who mattered ever missed them.

"This the one?" he asked pointing to Raissa in the corner. She and Monteñez were speaking the local Spanish dialect. Raissa knew about ten to fifteen words in that language. She had no idea what they were saying.

"Yes. And it breaks my heart to give her to you."

"Don't fret, Esmerita" he retorted, his eyes pinned to the naked buttocks of his new toy. "There's always cunt around."

"Yes," the woman said. "And cocks to fill them."

Monteñez laughed. "I want to see her tits," he said. "Tell her to turn around and come here."

"Raissa," Esmeralda called to the naked girl in English. "Please come here and meet Señor Monteñez."

The Russian girl walked timidly forward. She had heard the man's rough voice behind her. She knew that she had been called up to Madam's room for some special reason because by now she would usually be getting ready for the evening customers. She looked at him cautiously. She hoped that he wouldn't beat her.

Esmeralda turned to Monteñez and started to say, "This is Raissa...."

The giant man had already taken a step towards the girl. He grabbed her breasts with both hands. Raissa stepped back in surprise. He responded by closing his thumbs and forefingers over her nipples and squeezing them hard.

"Ohhhhh!" Raissa exclaimed. The man lifted his hands high forcing Raissa's nipples to extend until she had to step up on her toes. "Ohhhhh!" she complained again.

"Don't walk away from me, cunt," Monteñez said to her.

"She doesn't speak Spanish," Esmeralda told him.

"She knows what I'm saying," he replied ominously.

Raissa's eyes looked desperately over at her mistress. "You're not going to make me fuck him?" they said.

The big man clamped his bear sized hands over Raissa's breasts. "Hmmmmm," he murmured. "Nice. Let's see the cunt." He pushed the girl over to a settee and sat her down in it. He raised her knees and admired her bare pussy lips. "Nice. Good choice, Esmerita."

"About the other ones, who did you pick?"

"There was a Brazilian girl and these two white girls. I think your people said that they were Canadian."

"Your mother's a whore!" Esmeralda exclaimed. "You can't have them! You just can't have them! I just bought them yesterday!"

"Then you should have bought them tomorrow," Monteñez laughed. "I'm taking them."

"I can't run a whorehouse like this. All of the best girls…"

Monteñez fixed a deadly glare on her. "I'll pick who I want, bitch!" he said angrily. "And you know why!"

The senior partner in the establishment used Monteñez' ranch as a refueling point for planes carrying cocaine being ferried north. It was an important link in a 200 million dollar a year enterprise, net. Four whores was just part of the price. This year. Greedy people tended to find themselves lying face down in their soup in this business.

"Be careful, Esmerita," the huge, barbarous looking man threatened. "Next year I might pick you."

Esmeralda quailed at the suggestion. She tried another tack. "Didn't any others of our trained whores strike your fancy? There's the American girl, Maureen."

"With the brown hair and fat tits? You've got to be kidding. My boys would put a hog's nose on her and make her crawl around like a pig!" He laughed again. "No, I've made my decision. My truck will be here in about an hour. Make sure the girls get good and comfy."

Esmeralda resigned herself to defeat. When the time came, she would like to have the opportunity to spit into this man's grave.

Raissa was still sitting on the couch, the back of her knees still in Monteñez' hands. She was trembling, panicked at the big man's evil tone and the mistress's unmistakable fear of him. "What is happening?" she thought to herself.

"Let me explain to her...." Esmeralda started to say, pointing at the young girl.

"You don't have to explain anything to her," Monteñez interrupted. "I'm taking her with me now."

"Now?" Esmeralda said in surprise.

"Yeah, I'll put her in the trunk of my car."

"In the trunk?"

"Mind your own business you stupid whore," Monteñez spat out at the startled madam. "She's my cunt now and I'll do what I want with her."

Monteñez threw Raissa's legs down to the floor. He reached over and grabbed a big clump of her hair and dragged her to her feet.

"Ohhhh!" Raissa cried.

Monteñez slapped her face brutally twice. "Shut up!" he roared.

Raissa's eyes grew wide with fright. What was happening here? The man pulled her by her hair to the middle of the room. He reached into his pocket and pulled out what looked like a pair of pliers. He circled Raissa's neck with his other arm. He bent her in half so that her face was level with his waist.

"Don't do that here!" Esmeralda cried out. "You'll get blood everywhere."

"Fuck you, Esmeralda," Monteñez said. "You just don't want to see what going to happen to your little beauty right in front of you. You want it done way off in the mountains where you never have to see her again. So fuck you."

Raissa knew that something terrible was going to happen. She struggled futilely in the big man's grasp. Her bound hands twisted to get free. She saw his hand with the tool in it reach towards her face. Its pincers nestled in her nose. Then she felt stabbing, piercing pain. Monteñez had punched a large hole through the wall between her nostrils. It started bleeding profusely. "Ohhhhhhh!" was all Raissa could say, all she had said since she met this cruel man. Monteñez put the tool back in his pocket and produced a styptic pencil. He shoved it into the hole in Raissa's nose. She screamed as the acerbic paste spread over the torn skin, sealing off the flow of blood. She tried to tug her head out of Monteñez's grip. He just tightened it. The back end of her body was jumping up and down, but her head stood stock still.

Next, Monteñez brought out a large, bright, golden ring from his pocket. It had a small opening where the metal did not meet. Holding the girl's head still, he fitted the ring into the hole in her nose. The girl screamed and moaned at the pain. "Stop! Please stop!" she yelled in Russian. "You're killing me! For the love of God, stop!"

But Monteñez had the ring through the hole already. The gap in the ring was turned to the outside. He took one more tool out of his pocket and put its pincers on either side of the ring's opening and squeezed. He had mighty hands and was able to close the gap on the ring easily. The ends married perfectly and clicked together. He put the tool away and turned the ring until the joinder was inside Raissa's nose.

Monteñez pulled Raissa's head up by her hair, displaying her new jewelry. "Looks good, eh?" he asked Esmeralda. The golden ring hung down over her upper lip. There was deep red blood on her face, around her mouth, flowing down over her chin. She was giving the mistress a woeful look.

Raissa was crying and sniffling. She was holding back her sobs because she was afraid that the man would hit her again. The pain in her nose was excruciating. She had no illusions now. Her mistress had given her to this brutish man. "Oh, God," she thought. "Please, no, please."

Monteñez circled his finger through the ring. The pressure brought new tears to Raissa's eyes. "Adios," he said to Esmeralda. "See you in the fall. I'll come here and try out some of your new whores." Monteñez laughed as he pulled Raissa by her nose out the door. Raissa was crying and moaning in pain as she followed him, naked, her hands twisting behind her. Esmeralda could hear her muffled screams and cries of dismay after her door was closed as Monteñez led her down the hall. Finally, her sounds grew quieter and then ended. The beautiful Russian girl was gone.

Esmeralda gave a big sigh. "Oh well," she thought. It was a waste of good flesh; that was what bothered her the most. And the fucking guy didn't even pay for her! Esmeralda had an investment in that whore. She picked up the phone and dialed a number.

"Hello, is Paolo there?.... Thanks.' She waited a few minutes.

"Paolo," a voiced said.

"Paolo, hello. This is Esmeralda. How are you?"

"Fine conchita, and you?"

"Fine, fine," she responded to the pleasant greeting.

"Those products that you spoke to me about last week, are they still available?....No?....Too bad.....Next week. Good, sure.....I'll fly up. Okay. Bye."

More product next week. Who knows, maybe another beautiful Russian or a Czech. A tourist? Well, someone's fate hung in the balance. Somewhere out there were young women walking around carefree and happy. In a week, that will seem a distant past to them, she thought to herself.

She would go downstairs and see what could be done about stretching the whores out a little. She was down two working girls. The Canadians hadn't been trained yet and so they wouldn't be missed right away. Then there was the fat girl, Maureen. Well, it was unfair to call her fat, but she was certainly big boned. She couldn't help it. In fact, she showed all the signs of having lost a lot of weight recently, dark rings around her eyes, excess, flabby skin around her hips.

When Esmeralda walked into the reception room, the place where the men selected their companions, the room seemed empty. It was early yet. If only the mayor's party finished soon. Perhaps she could create a municipal crises and he would have to run out, she laughed to herself. She could see him running down the street holding his hat with one hand on his head and his pants around his ankles.

She was mistaken. The room was not empty. Maureen was sitting alone in the corner. She was naked from the waist up, showing off her big, fluffy breasts. But her broad shoulders too. She was wearing a flowered peasant skirt that hid her football player's thighs. What would she ever do with her?

Alessandro was behind the bar. She asked for tequila and a lime. "You too," she told him.

The bartender poured two generous shots of tequila and he and his boss shot them back. Esmeralda nodded at Maureen. "No luck, eh?"

"Would you want her if you could have one of the other girls? Where'd you get her anyway?" the bartender asked. They had been together for many years. Alessandro kept a Glock behind the bar for emergencies.

"She was part of a package deal. Her and two Russians," Esmeralda replied. "Now I've got her and one Russian who speaks no English and no Spanish."

"Well, frankly, I think she looks like a pig."

"What did you say?" Esmeralda asked him. She had been deep in thought.

"She looks like a pig, you know, oink, oink." At this sound, Maureen turned her head. She saw that they were both looking at her. She knew that the oink reference was probably for her. Life as a whore in El Papaya was not all peaches and cream. Some of the men here were nice, but some beat her and a few rather badly. She had gotten used to that. But she didn't like being called a pig. She had had enough of that in high school. She wasn't a pig. She couldn't help her bone structure.

Esmeralda had turned her head to Alessandro. He continued, amused at her reaction. "You know, you should stick a hog's nose on her and make her run around on all fours. The customers will get a big kick out of it."

Esmeralda laughed. "That's exactly what Monteñez said. Put a pig's nose on her. We could do that."

"Seriously?" Alessandro asked, intrigued.

"Seriously," the madam replied. She looked at Maureen. "First thing tomorrow," she thought.

The next morning, Maureen was brought upstairs to Esmeralda's boudoir. She had been brought up naked with her hands tied behind her back. It was standard for all of the inmates of 'El Papaya' to be bound when they traveled throughout the house. Maureen was escorted by Cesar, who was the head of security and one of the house's main trainers. He had a mean streak a mile wide.

"What's this about a pig?" he asked his titular boss. Cesar was never bossed around by anyone.

"Yes," Esmeralda answered. "Since she is such a lousy whore, maybe we can entertain the guests a little. I mean who's ever fucked a real pig? Here, put this on her nose."

Esmeralda held out a plastic pig's nose with an elastic band fixed to it. She had had one of the towel boys run out to a costume shop that morning. Maureen was standing next to Cesar and saw it. Her heart sunk. They <u>were</u>

talking about her yesterday when they made the 'oinking' sounds. She felt a tear coming on.

Cesar wrapped the elastic band around Maureen's head and placed the plastic pig's nose over her natural one. Both he and Esmeralda immediately laughed. "That's it! That's it!" the madam managed to shout out behind her laughter. Cesar was laughing too. Maureen started to cry. "Why are they making fun of me?" she thought. "I've done everything they said."

"Ha, ha, ha, ha, ha," Esmeralda could not control her laughter. "M,make her say 'oink'," she cried out. She was nearly doubled over.

Cesar, his mirth evident in his voice told the unhappy girl in English, "Say 'oink'."

Maureen looked at him like he was crazy. Why would they do this, she thought. Cesar pushed her shoulder firmly. His voice was more serious now.

"I said, 'say oink'."

Maureen looked miserably at the still giggling madam. Grimacing, knowing what would happen, she let the hated sound pass over her lips. "Oink," she said sullenly.

Then pair broke out into raucous laughter. Maureen just stood there as the two slavers had the time of their life at her expense. "I've got to get Alessandro up here," Esmeralda managed to get out. "I got the idea from him."

By the time Alessandro had come up, Maureen was down on her hands and knees. Cesar had taught her how to grunt. When Alessandro saw her face, he too burst out laughing. "It's too much," he cried. "She looks just like a pig!"

"Well, we've got to fatten her up!" Esmeralda said when she had gained control of herself. Hearing Maureen grunt had set her off all over again. "I want to get special shoes for her hands and something for her knees. From today, she never gets on two legs. I want thirty pounds on her in two weeks." The conscienceless madam paused. She tried to suppress another outbreak of mirth. "And I want her to get a tail!" All three of them set off on another round of unrestrained laughter.

Before she left, Maureen's legs were brought up behind her and taped off to her thighs. They taped some pads to her knees. And they left the nose on. Maureen cried and cried as Cesar led her back downstairs. He took her down the elevator.

From that day on, Maureen lived her life as a pig. If she refused to eat, she was force fed, a steel tube thrust down her throat, pureed food poured in, creamy desserts, fatty meats, bacon. That last set off more laughter. She no longer was allowed to sleep in the whore's dorm, but they had converted a closet into a kind of sty. Her head was shaved. She was never allowed to stand or stretch her legs.

Maureen was kept away from the guests. Her appearance was to be a big surprise. After three weeks, Maureen had put on about thirty pounds. They had had made a pair of black, shiny, shoe like gloves for her hands, pointy, like a pig's hoof. It was getting harder and harder to fasten her legs to her thighs as she put on weight, but they managed. Esmeralda hired a makeup artist to show one of her staff how to make up a pig's nose so it looked real and stuck to her face without an elastic band. The artist fashioned a pair of pointy pig's ears. And there was the tail. A six inch, windey, spring like tail. Cesar, who was the house specialist on piercing, had figured out how to lay a flat metal bar under her skin just above her rectum. The tail had a little clip on the end and, when pressed into the plate, it lodged solidly in. It could not be removed unless the plate was removed too. He also added a large, gold ring to her nose.

And so she was ready for her debut. They always had a big party on the Cinqo de Mayo. The whole city did. The whole country. They planned to bring her out that night. Many of the notables had made reservations for 'El Papaya's' after party party. It started about 1 a.m.

Esmeralda had borrowed a few girls from a neighboring house and there was plenty of cunt to go around. The party was held in the main ballroom and the price of sex was included in the price of admission.

Many of the wealthy patrons of the house were there. Some had brought their mistresses, promising them a delicious pussy to eat. There was a mariachi band, of course, and a modern Latino jazz trio. There was booze and plenty of lewd entertainment. Each working girl had to spend at least twenty minutes on one of the three small stages caressing herself for the benefit of the audience.

A little after two o'clock, Esmeralda shushed everybody in order to make an announcement. 'Gentlemen and ladies, I have promised you all a big surprise tonight. In keeping with my pledge, I am honored to bring to you one of the Seven Wonders of the World, La Taconera Cochina!"

Esmeralda stepped aside with a flourish of her hands. The crowd applauded and the band struck up an old mariachi song called, "Kick the Pig". Two tall, muscular, naked black men came in pulling a large flatbed cart. It was bedecked with Mexican Flags and red, white and green ribbons. In the middle, with a necklace of bright red flowers around her neck was Maureen, La Taconera Cochina, literally the whore pig. Maureen knelt on all fours on the platform. Her thirty pounds had made a huge difference and her flesh was beginning to bulge everywhere. Her legs were tied to her thighs and wrapped with heavy, flesh colored gauze that covered even her feet, so that they would not detract from the illusion. But it was her face outfitted with the little pig nostrils, the hairy, pointed ears, and the tail, that made it. She looked like she had been transformed by Circe herself. To top it off, there were a dozen tiny piglets on the moveable stage, running back and forth, giving off their little squeals.

Maureen was beyond mortification. She had given up all her hopes of humane treatment as soon as they had made her crawl around the floor oinking and grunting like a pig. Her nightmare of her whole youth had come true. She was a pig, she thought. She had been hiding under the skin of a young woman, but these cruel people had smoked her out. She didn't cry, she didn't protest. Her eyes misted, but she held her tears back. "Pigs don't cry," she told herself.

The black men pulled the stage into the middle of the room. One of the men jumped up onto it and released all the little pigs. They leapt off of the stage and began to run around the room to everyone's delight. The man took a position behind Maureen's rear. This was the moment that Maureen feared. They had been working on her all week. Every two hours or so, while she was held in a little room with straw on the floor, someone came by to stroke her to orgasm. She would moan and groan wildly as her body convulsed with pleasure. And when someone wasn't stimulating her to orgasm with their hand, they were fucking her, front and back. She grew to need it, to want it. Her cunt began to dilate the moment that someone opened the door. She had even learned how to raise her head so that her snout did not get in the way of giving oral gratification.

And they had tried something special on her yesterday. Cesar came in with a hyperemic needle. He had terrorized her for three weeks, beating her at least once every day. She meekly let him raise her head and carefully plunge the hypo into her throat and into her vocal chords. There was no effect for about an hour. Then Esmeralda and Alessandro came in with Cesar to test the results of the experiment. Esmeralda stood behind her and began to caress her sex. Maureen responded immediately. Her pussy grew moist and hot, her nipples hardened. Esmeralda was driving her towards completion of her lust. She moaned. And then it happened. Instead of a low, guttural moan, a moan of a woman in passion, her voice emerged in a tiny wheeze, not unlike a squeal. Esmeralda and the men burst into laughter. The madam did not pause in her torment of Maureen's cunt. The poor girl could not help herself and she groaned and moaned as she came, filling the room with high pitched squeals. The experiment had been a resounding success!

The ballroom was full of uncontrolled laughter. Maureen was the hit of the party. The black man placed his hand between her thighs from behind. A spotlight was shined on the stage. He began to worry her little pleasure bud. Tears flowing down her face, Maureen could not hold back her arousal. Her nose ring was tied to a post on the stage so that she could not even hide her head in shame. She tried to hold back, she fought it with all her might, but the man's hand expertly stroked her pussy's lips, relentlessly tickled her swollen clit. When he sensed Maureen getting close to orgasm, he raised his free hand to quiet the crowd. The room was absolutely silent. Maureen's panting breath could be heard by those close to the stage. And then, she was pushed over the top. She groaned loudly as sharp pulses of pleasure flowed through her, pleasure that she didn't want. "Wheeeeeeou! Wheeeeeeou!" she called out. The crowd exploded in laughter. Maureen wanted to die of shame. But she could not hold back as the hand coaxed more explosive contractions from her womb. "Wheeeeeou! Wheeeeeeeeeou!"

And then she felt the black man's hot meat slide into her blossomed pussy. After almost nonstop sex for the past week, Maureen had been left to burn since that morning, with someone coming in and manipulating her to excitement at regular intervals, but stopping before she reached her crest. Her need was upon her and she blocked out all but the thick, hard dick that was plowing her cunt. "Wheeeeeou! Wheeeeeou!" she called out as she continued to come. It did not take long for the black man to orgasm and he was replaced by the other. This one chose her narrower passage and made her moan with pain as he jammed himself in. Again she squealed loudly, this time in pain rather than pleasure. There was laughter all around as the crowd witnessed Maureen's degradation. When the second tall, well built, black man was done, he unleashed her nose ring and, lowering a ramp, led her onto the floor. The band started up to playing again. People gathered around the pig whore, feeling her sloppy pussy, grabbing her huge tits that hung down below her chest. Some of the men decided to fuck her and there was a cheer every time one of them made her squeal. Two of the women, not whores, guests, crawled under her rotund belly and began to suck on her teats while one of the men was fucking her. Maureen's mind went blank as another almost crippling orgasm tore through her. "Wheeeeeeuo! Wheeeeeeeou!" she cried out.

As Esmeralda watched the crowd enjoy themselves with La Taconera Cochina, the pig whore, she knew that many of those present tonight would come back to hear her squeal like a pig again, and many more would come who had missed out on La Taconera Cochina's debut. She placed her hand on her hip as she watched a man stuff his prick into Maureen's squealing mouth. "If there's one thing I know," she said to herself, "it's how to make money from a whore."

CHAPTER TWO
JAKE SEARCHES FOR A PONY GIRL

The copper colored Range Rover had been following the winding and heavily potholed dirt road for about twenty miles. To Jake, the trip along the rolling hills of the central Kalikastan plains seemed to be interminable. Due to the meandering road and its poor condition, they were rarely able to achieve more than 50 kilometers per hour. It was lucky that they had the Range Rover since in places over their two week trip the roads had been washed out by the near torrential late spring rains. Sitting next to Jake in the driver's seat was a short, lean, blond bearded man, about 45 years of age. His name was Irkut and he was acting as Jake's guide and interpreter. He was well versed in the niceties of ponygirl flesh, having acted as a trainer for many years. Now he acted as a kind of broker for those estates that trained ponygirls commercially.

Kalikastan is a wide open, kind of Wild West country in which the rich and powerful have revived the ancient custom of breaking suitable young women into servile and sexually available ponygirls. Deprived of voice and identity through the ever-present hoods and gags they are forced to wear, the ponygirls serve as sexual playthings and are in high demand. But the main purpose of owning ponygirls is to race them. Ponygirl tournaments are held in the interior of the country between wealthy estates throughout the spring, culminating in a grand tournament at the end of the six week racing season. The hot, dry summers being deemed inappropriate for the rigors of racing, another six week season commences in late August running into October.

In order to establish their caché as evildoers, Jake and Burnham had devised a scheme in which they took control of the New Jersey slavery operation. It had supplied a steady stream of nubile, young girls to the Kalikastan slave market. Jake's team was charged with continuing the operation as a source of contact with the Kalikastani slavers. Burnham, as the new principal of the slaving operation in the States, had then bribed his way into obtaining several huge international construction contracts for oil and gas pipelines through the strategically located country. Based on his promises of contributing a vast amount of graft, the National Commission, a loosely assembled council of major organized crime leaders, had granted him ownership of his own estate in the Kalikastan hinterland, one formerly owned by an aspiring Russian crime lord who had stepped on too many toes. The Commission had 'dissolved" the errant crime lord's nascent organization, liquidated the principal, shipped his wife and daughters off to a Middle Eastern slave dealer and confiscated the estate. Based on the immense largess that Burnham promised to bring into their coffers, they agreed to make him an honorary Kalikastan citizen.

Jake's present task was to populate the empty ponygirl barn on Burnham's estate, the previous stock having been confiscated by the Commission. He had been on the road for the better part of two weeks obstensively in pursuit of promising ponygirls who would be melded into Burnham's racing teams. Irkut had been retained to act as Burnham's trainer and procurer. So far, Jake and Irkut had visited seven different estates and purchased six pony girls. Today they would be visiting their eighth.

What Irkut did not know was that Jake was on the lookout for Burnham's niece, Maddy. It was like looking for a needle in a haystack. They did not know what estate had purchased Maddy and the slave center where they processed her would certainly not tell them. Transactions involving female slavery were naturally highly confidential and anybody asking about them would be dealt with in a forthright and permanent manner. There were hundreds of ponygirls spread out over dozens of estates small and large throughout the country. Even if Jake happened on the estate that owned Maddy, it would be extremely difficult to pick her out from all the others. The faces of ponygirls were never exposed. Other than for cleaning purposes, they were condemned at all times to wearing a tight fitting neoprene hood over their head, obscuring all identity, even to themselves. Their bodies were rendered hairless other than a long, thick strand gathered in a ponytail at the back of their heads which was allowed to drape out of a hole in the back of the hood. True, Jake had a good idea of Maddy's size and physical dimensions, and he knew her hair color, a deep reddish brown. But almost all of the ponygirls were of the same general body type: tall, muscular, broad shouldered and with long legs and ample breasts.

There was one thing on Jake's side. Maddy was what was known as a yearling. This was the nickname for newly broken in ponygirls who were into their first racing season. It was virtually certain that Maddy would have been trained to race as a yearling. In the course of his ponygirl buying expedition, Jake was attending as many of the local estate races as he could. He had a picture of Maddy in a bikini taken from her apartment by him as part of the investigation into her kidnapping. There was a small mole on Maddy's right hip. If he could get close enough to see her, Jake just might be able to pick her out.

It had not rained now for several days and the Range Rover left a large cloud of dust behind it as it raced along the narrow dirt road. Suddenly, the road veered to the left away from the river and they entered what appeared to be a long, dirt driveway bordered by high, white, rail fences, the kind you see on horse farms. There were, in fact, several horses lolling on the neatly trimmed grass. After a mile or so, the road led to a large, white, wooden gateway with a long, high, white wooden gate. Atop the gate was a painted heraldic shield with a golden winged dragon atop a field of blue. Under the shield in large, black italic script was the motto, *"Vigilantia. Robur. Voluptas."* Jake's recollection of his high school Latin allowed him to decipher it. "Vigilance. Strength. Pleasure." He smiled as he thought, "But whose pleasure?"

The range Rover crawled to a stop and a heavy set elderly man, with a long white beard and stark, blue eyes emerged from a little gatehouse. He took his time walking over to the driver's side of the car, yawning and scratching his jellied paunch. When he reached Irkut's window, he issued a loud grunt.

"Greetings, grandfather," Irkut said to the old man in Russian.

"Greetings yourself," the man replied saucily. "You must be lost comrade, this is not a hotel."

"Don't comrade me, uncle," Irkut retorted. "Those days are over."

"Bah!" the old man exclaimed. "And a shame it is too! I had a pension, health care, a fine little apartment and no worries. Now look at me. I'm nothing more than a wage slave to these mafiamen. If only Comrade Stalin was alive…."

"Enough of the reminiscing, Uncle," Irkut spat out, interrupting the old man's reverie. "We're new men and we're here to see your boss. I'll put in a good word for your diligence at keeping out the riffraff."

The old man's eyes lit up and a mischievous smirk spread across his face. "You here to see the ponygirls?" he asked, his voice friendly and interested.

"You should have been a detective, grandfather, or maybe an agent of state security. Of course we're here for the ponygirls," Irkut told him. "I've got a suitcase full of euros here and I'm sure your boss would like some of them. Let us in before we become statues here."

"Oh, yes, oh, yes," the man exclaimed. "The race is tomorrow. Big party tonight. I'll phone up to the main house." The old man scurried to the gatehouse and Jake heard him talking into the telephone. He had understood nothing of the banter between Irkut and the gatekeeper, but had come to accept that nobody did anything in this country without having a little chat first. The old man came out a few moments later waving his hands and trotted over to the side of the gate. He unlocked it and swung it open. Irkut slowly edged the Range Rover forward and handed a five Euro note to the old man.

"For your pension, grandfather," he yelled as he stepped on the gas. Jake could see the old man waiving and smiling in the side view mirror as they pulled away.

The driveway continued for another mile before it reached the top of a small rise. There were several large wooden barns, a barracks like building and a huge, stone mansion. In the middle of all of the buildings was a large racing track surrounded by the ubiquitous white railings. Jake observed several hooded ponygirl teams out there being put through their paces. He could see them leaning forwards, naked, their hands bound behind them, straining to pull their carriages or carts. Their ponytails bounced behind their bobbing heads and their bare breasts jiggled as they ran. Their stiff, black leather boots stirred up the dusty surface as they drove their toes deeply into the dirt for traction. A small audience of idle men dressed in black jeans and black polo shirts sat on the rail calling out jests and encouragement to the forlorn young females.

The Range Rover turned into a courtyard that lay in front of the stone mansion. There were several large, black Mercedes parked there. Two men holding automatic rifles paced the gravel pathway that led around the house. The presence of the armed men did not faze Jake as he knew that all of the estates were constantly on guard against 'incursions' by rival organizations. There were six main criminal 'families' in the country and they conducted a constant undeclared war against each other. The only place that was off limits to this struggle for wealth and power was the capital, Dlitski. It was an open city and no violence was tolerated there.

Irkut guided the utility vehicle to a halt and the two men stepped out. The sky was bright and clear and the early afternoon sun glared off of the large, white double doors that served as the main entrance and the wide wooden steps that led up to it. Irkut nodded to Jake and the two men began to ascend the steps. The front door opened as they reached the top and a thin, officious, bald headed man appeared. He was dressed in a dark blue suit with a narrow black tie over a white shirt. His shoes were of shiny patent leather. He had a thin moustache over his upper lip. He held his hand out to Irkut and gave him a thin, wan smile.

"Greetings, you old pirate," he said in Russian. "I see you've brought the American cowboy with you."

"Fuck you, Leonid," Irkut replied in English as he gave him a hearty handshake. "Speak English for my guest."

"Of course," Leonid said, also in English. He looked at Jake. "My pleasure," he said, holding out his hand. "You are Mr. Barnes, I presume. Welcome to our estate."

Jake had picked up on the tall man's contemptuous greeting to Irkut. He decided to let it go. "The pleasure's all mine," he said as he shook Leonid's hand.

"Mr. Gregarov is out riding. Please come in and have some tea while you wait for him," Leonid offered. Pavlov Gregarov was a major player in Kalikastan. His was one of the larger estates, funded through 'insurance' paid to him by many of the prosperous but vulnerable young corporations of the new Russian and Ukrainian Republics. He also had vast sums of money 'on the street' and enforced the onerous interest rates he charged ruthlessly. He spent most of his time back in Moscow and Kiev, but liked to get away to his estate whenever he could. During racing season, he spent almost all of his time there.

Jake and Irkut were led into the foyer of the huge, red granite house. It was an unlikely construction style for the middle of what was essentially a steppe, but Gregarov had once seen a picture of a 500 year old English manorial house and had copied it to a 'T'. The foyer bespoke his immense wealth and gaudy taste. Flags and shield and suits of armor lined the walls. The floor was white marble. A white marble staircase wound up to the upper floors.

Leonid led the men into a vast receiving room to the right of the foyer. The room had a dark maroon rug and several long, brown, leather couches. Black glass topped coffee tables sat in front of each one. At Leonid's invitation, Jake and Irkut took a seat. There was a diminutive young woman standing by one of the ceiling high French windows. She was naked but for a wide, bright red belt and a long, blood red fabric draped over the belt and down to her feet. It was narrow enough so that the outside of her milk white thighs could be seen. She was barefooted and wore her jet black hair in a long braid down her back. Her breasts were invitingly plump and firm. She stood there in front of the tall, tan drapes, her head down, her hands behind her back.

"Tea," Leonid barked to her in English. The girl jumped at the sound of his voice and ran out of the room, a long swath of red fabric trailing behind her. While the girl fetched the tea, Jake took the time to examine the room. The walls were mauve and there was a vast chandelier in the middle of the ceiling. On the wall to the left of the door, over a dominating, rough hewn stone fireplace, was a 25' square oil painting. It depicted what appeared to be a charge of eighteenth century Cossack cavalry. Madly angry, coarsely dressed, bearded men, their bright sabers lifted before them, urged their demonic steeds forwards. The men were depicted from the front and it looked like the Cossacks were about to pour into the room through the wall. It was the kind of thing that made you understand why men holding muzzle loading, short range muskets would have thrown them away and run.

The dark haired girl returned accompanied by three other similarly clad women. Each was holding a silver tray containing respectively a brace of tea cups, a large, silver urn, sugar and milk and an assortment of honey covered pastries and cookies. The women were all young and beautiful and, after delivering their wares, knelt in a line in front of the coffee table in display for the benefit of the two guests, their hands behind their backs and their eyes downcast. Each wore the distinctive blue shield of the estate with its bright yellow, fearsome dragon tattooed on their bellies. Cyrillic writing adorned their chests above their breasts which Jake had learned denoted, in Russian, the names that had been assigned to them soon after their enslavement. Black leather collars and bracelets adorned all of their necks, wrists and ankles.

Leonid took the liberty of pouring the tea. "May I present Klara, Lana, Dalia and Veronica. They will be happy to entertain you while you wait for the Master." The tall, thin man snapped his fingers and the four voluptuous women scurried to the middle of the room. As one, they removed their wide, red leather belts and let the draping fabric fall to the floor. Without fanfare, they paired off and began kissing and caressing each other.

Jake had eyes for the lithe, long haired, blond girl. He watched, almost mesmerized as the brunette with whom she had paired off drank at her full, plush lips. The girls were both kneeling and their torsos were pressed firmly together, their bounteous breasts mashed against each other's. Their hands worked each other's backs and thighs as their mouths locked feverishly together. The blond girl took the brunette's head in her hands and pulled her own head back so that her tongue could be seen dancing over and between the brunette's lips. Slowly, the blond edged the brunette to the floor and lay atop her, insinuating her long, graceful leg between her thighs.

Next to the blond and brunette, the black haired girl was on her back, her legs spread wide. Her partner, a fiery looking red head, had her hands on the girl's widespread thighs and was supping at the black haired girl's wide open cleft. As the men sipped their tea, the room was silent except for the moans of the women and the sound of lips sucking against flesh. The girls were all clean shaven below and Jake could see the gleaming slit of the blond girl as she too began to gemauch her partner. She was kneeling between the other girl's legs and was bent to her task. Her legs were spread wide and several long fingers from her right hand were worrying her own pleasure bud.

Leonid's strategy was clear. In a short while, he and Irkut would be viewing the naked bodies of dehumanized females with an eye to a purchase of one or two of them. Being sexually aroused without satisfaction would make them just that much more ready to make a buy. It was traditional that a ponygirl's new owner take her sexually right on the spot and having a need to get off would make a sale that much more likely. The strategy was working as Jake took note of his hardened cock.

"If you are in the market for household slaves," Leonid stated, breaking momentarily the spell cast by the fornicating women, "these slaves are all newly trained. They have come from our facility in Dlitski just this week. I can assure you that they are well disciplined and very compliant.

"Well...," Jake thought. They would need to stock up on house slaves. And having a ready mouth and cunt along for the ride in the Range Rover might make the driving much more interesting. He would give it some consideration.

Just then, the girls on their backs both began to sigh and moan. The topmost girls, as if on signal, slid their bodies around so that their long, agile tongues approached the pussies of their partners from above. They spread their charges' thighs wide, giving the men a full view of their gushing slits. The black haired girl came first, her thighs shuddering, her hips rocking. "Oh! Oh! Oh!" she called out as the redhead tormented her pleasure bud with her tongue. Just as the black haired girl's spasms began to subside, the brunette took her turn and began to buck and quake under the body of the blonde who lay diagonally across her torso. The blonde used her fingers to spread the brunette's labia wide and she dragged her long, pink tongue the length of the slit between them. Jake watched as she buried her tongue deeply into the writhing girl's crevasse. The brunette moaned loudly and screamed, "Uhhhhhhhhh! Uhhhhhhhhhhh!" as her orgasm tore through her.

The black haired girl and the redhead had changed positions. The black haired girl, Veronica, had spun the redheaded girl around so that she was on her back, her head towards the guests. She grabbed the redhead's legs from behind the knees and began to push them over her torso, bending the shapely, young slave girl in two. Then, pressing her chest and stomach against the redhead's back, she presented the redhead's moist gash to the now lustful men. Keeping the redhead's legs splayed and bent over towards the mesmerized men, Veronica began to stroke the dripping pussy, spreading its folds, teasing the little nubbin at its apex.

In the meantime, the blonde and the brunette had also exchanged places. The blonde was on her hands and knees facing the men. Her plump bosoms hung below her chest like ripe fruit. The brunette knelt next to her and pried open her hairless pussy from behind with her left hand. With her right, she began to caress and stroke the blond haired girl's beauteous, pale globes, teasing the hardened nipples, squeezing the breasts with her full hand. The blond haired girl's head was up and she was looking directly at Jake and Irkut. Her face was a mask of passion as she endured the pleasurable ministrations of the other girl.

Jake knew which one he would pick if given the choice. He had a thing for blondes and this girl, with her pleasantly round face, slim nose, large, candid eyes, was one of the most beautiful he had seen. Her hair was back behind her in a braid just like the black haired girl's. Jake watched as she licked and then bit her lips as her lust heightened. This time she was first and her face contorted with obvious paroxysms of pleasure. Her body shook and she began to rock back and forth on her knees, causing her orbs to sway to and fro beneath her. Keeping her mouth tightly closed, jamming her eyes shut, the blond seemed to be trying to fight off the inevitable crescendo of pleasure she was undergoing. "Mmmmmmmpf! Mmmmmmmpf!" she moaned as she tried to suppress her exclamations of fleshly delight. "Mmmmmmmmpf!"

The redheaded girl soon followed suit. Her cunt was dripping wet and the black haired girl had her whole fist buried in it. She pumped steadily at the redheaded girl's trough who was giving out little cries. "Ah! Ah! Ah! Ah!"

Suddenly she was over the top. "Aaaaaaa! Ah! Ah! Ah! Ahhhhhhhhhh!" she cried out as the jolts of pleasure coursed through her. Her feet were in the air above her face and they jerked back and forth as she orgasmed.

When the girls were done, they sheepishly resumed their obsequious positions before the men. Their faces showed the evidence of their spent passions and their bodies gleamed with perspiration. The blond girl and the redhead were struggling to regain their breath.

A loud clapping came from the doorway to the lounge. Jake and Irkut turned their heads as one and saw a large, broad shouldered man dressed in heavy, brown corduroy work pants, black boots and a white peasant style shirt. He had a thick, wild, black beard and blazing eyes. "Ho, ho!" he cried out while smashing his palms together loudly. "Very good! Very good!"

Jake and Irkut rose from the sofa. Leonid's posture stiffened and his contemptuous stare softened into a more compliant demeanor. "Mr. Gregarov," he said politely and formally, "may I present Mr. Irkut Tamminov and Mr. Jake Barnes. He is the American we spoke about."

Gregarov strode into the room. He seemed as big as a house. "My pleasure gentlemen, my pleasure," he said as he held out his hand. He shook both Jake's and Irkut's hands. His paw was as mighty as a bear's and just as hairy. Jake noticed that there was a Colt .45 strapped to his waist and a long quirt in his left hand. Gregarov took in Jake's observation of his sidearm and whip. "A good American pistol," he said. "Anything you hit will go right down. And the quirt is for my racing team, a six pony cabriolet. Come on out, I'll show you."

Jake and Irkut polished off their cups of tea and followed the lumbering gangster outside. Standing in the courtyard in front of the white wooden stairs was a fine, black leather covered cabriolet with four large wheels. In front of it, hitched together and linked to the carriage were six, naked, hooded females.

The ponies wore dull red, almost maroon, hoods that obscured their entire head and face except for a hole for their mouth and two tiny apertures for their eyes. The hoods covered their necks as well, running down to their stiff, thick, leather collars, wider in front than in back so that their chins were held up and they all appeared to be looking up at the sky. The long hoods which covered their necks made it seem like their heads had sprung up out of their collars and were not part of their body. Jake could see the sweat pouring off of them and the dirt and dust spread over their torsos and legs. They were lined up in three rows of two. Their hips were attached to three long, wooden shafts, one in the middle running between each pair and one on either side of them. Leather straps connected from the harnesses they were all wearing to the front of the carriage.

Two long sets of reins ran the length of the line of hooded ponygirls to the two lead ponies and were fastened to their bits. The rest of the ponies wore leather shields across their lower faces undoubtedly attached to mouth filling gags. The wrists of all the ponies were confined behind their backs and their hands were covered with red leather mittens that matched their hoods.

But the most distinctive thing about these ponies was that they all had dark brown skin and jet black hair. Jake had been to a few estates and had seen a number of ponygirls race. Most of the females were pale skinned Caucasians with maybe a few light brown Hispanics or olive skinned Mediterranean females thrown in. But these females had been apparently purposely picked to be of dark hue and matching hair. They all seemed of the same height, about 5'11", and had similar builds. If not for the slight differences in the shape and sizes of their breasts, and these differences were not all that great, they could have been clones.

"You like my team?" Gregarov asked, inviting the obvious complement.

"Very nice," Irkut answered. "Mexican?"

"No," Gregarov replied. "Guatemalan. From up in the mountains. They grow them tall and strong up there."

Jake walked along the line of women appreciatively. They all stood stock still, like terra cotta figures. Six red hooded females, naked and bound, hitched to a carriage like real ponies: it was quite a sight. Jake stood in front of the lead ponygirls. He looked up at Gregarov. "May I?" he asked.

"Please yourself," Gregarov answered with a broad grin.

Jake cupped his palm under the breast of one of the lead girls. Her chest was still slightly heaving. He could just see the flicker of a brown eye behind one of the dime sized eyeholes of the hood. The breast was heavy and firm. He ran his thumb over the broad, fat nipple and it hardened obediently. "Very nice," he said. "Are they racing tomorrow?" he asked Gregarov.

"Of course," the large, muscular man said. "Andre Kamerov, who has an estate about 75 kilometers from here, should be here any time now. He's got a six pony team of Norwegian females. We're trying to interest the Commission in making purebred teams part of the Fall Tournament. There are about six or seven purebred teams working now. Next year I believe that there will be double that." Gregarov had strolled up next to Jake as he spoke and was standing next to him, stroking the hair of the lead pony whose breast was in Jake's hand.

"I've been working them to get ready for the race. They need to go back to the barn and get massaged and fed. I want them well rested for tomorrow."

Gregarov nodded to one of the grooms who was holding the bit of the front girl next to Jake. He began to pull on the bit and made a "tsch, tsch," sound. The ponygirls accepted this as the signal to move forward. Jake stepped back and let them proceed. The big, black, leather covered carriage came rolling past him. He watched silently as the six pony team walked gracefully away, their heavy boots clip clopping on the stone driveway.

"What do you say we get down to business, eh, gentlemen?" Gregarov asked. "I have a couple of yearlings and two or three older ponies that I think might interest you."

In Kalikastan, the ages of ponies were calculated from their date of capture. So a 24 year old girl who was new would be considered younger than a 22 year old who had been a pony for three years. The pony life took quite a toll on the females and any pony who had "chewed a bit" for more than six or seven years was considered too worn for racing. They might have a few more years of general purpose use, but the hard regimen of racing was considered beyond them. Of course there were exceptions, and some racing ponies lasted in the sport up to ten years, but these tended to be extraordinarily strong females with remarkable degrees of endurance.

Jake followed Irkut and Gregarov to the pony barn. Leonid trailed behind them all. It was a short walk and while they were walking, Jake saw some of the racing teams being pulled off of the track and led towards the barn. A couple of teams were still running languorous laps around the track, more to keep loose and toned than anything else.

The men spent the next hour in the barn examining five of Gregarov's ponies that he was offering for sale. Irkut had the knack of judging the "age" of the females by assessing their thighs and looking for wear from the bits they wore at the corner of their mouths. Two of the five were rejected, diplomatically, out of hand. That left two yearlings and one brown haired female that Gregarov maintained was, "a two year old." Jake needed to acquire some seasoned ponygirls so that the estate could field more teams than just yearlings. Besides, or so he was told, it helped the younger fillies to have the older, more trained ones to show them the way.

The three ponies were led out to the track. Irkut timed the two year old as she ran two laps at full speed. He was impressed. The first yearling to run, a black haired female, ran pretty good, or as well as could be expected as a pony new to her traces. The second one, a blonde, ran rather poorly. She seemed to lack coordination and was skittish. Irkut looked at Jake and shook his head. The three red hooded ponies were led to the front of the barn and the bargaining began. All of the talking in front of the ponies was done in Russian, a language which none of them understood. Jake kept his mouth shut; he had no idea what to say anyway.

Irkut ran his hands up and down the inner thighs of the black haired yearling and made some disparaging sounding remark. He pulled at the breasts of the two year old and felt the crease of her sex, looking for her responsiveness. He seemed satisfied. He did not need to see their faces. No one would ever see them anyhow. He stepped behind the blond female and stroked her haunches, measured her shoulders with his strong, gnarled hands. Jake noticed that the blonde was trembling. He guessed that she had been a pony no more than two or three weeks.

Finally, Irkut and Gregarov came to terms. They would buy the two year old and the brunette yearling. Their prices were €30,000 for the yearling, untrained as she was, and €37,500 for the fully trained two year old. Cash, of course. Irkut had whispered the proposed terms into Jake's ear. Jake nodded. "That seems fair to me," he said.

He realized his mistake as soon as he made it. Only Russian was spoken before the yearlings. The blond haired pony stiffened. Her head came alert. She started to whine and cry and tried to make human sounds from behind her bit. She actually stepped up to Jake and began to rub her body against his, her voice a pleading jumble of sounds.

As Jake stepped back, Leonid sprang into action. He grabbed the ponygirl by her tail and yanked her head back sharply. With one foot, he kicked the feet out under the desperately mewing female and she hit the ground with a loud 'thump'. He signaled to two grooms who had been standing by and uttered a command in Russian. One of them disappeared into the barn and quickly brought out two long ropes. While Leonid held the protesting ponygirl in place, his hand gripping her pony tail tightly, the grooms rushed up and grabbed the legs of the frantic pony and tied ends of the ropes around her ankles. They then dragged her by her feet over to the barn where two large brackets, about five feet apart jutted out. They threw the other ends of the ropes over the brackets and hauled the bond haired pony into the air. When her head was about two feet off of the ground, they tied off the ends of the rope onto hitches.

The forlorn ponygirl hung suspended in the air upside down, her legs spread wide, her hands firmly fastened behind her back. She was facing the small group of men and was still struggling and screaming behind her bit. Her hooded head swung back and forth and her breasts jiggled wildly. Leonid knelt down by the ponygirl's head and uttered some soothing sounding words in Russian. He ran his hands over her breasts and then, standing, caressed her snow white, widespread thighs. He placed his hand on her hairless mound and pinched the pony's plump labia together hard until the pony began to jerk her legs and moan from the pain. Jake knew that this was just a tease. This ponygirl was in for a whopper of a beating.

One of the grooms, who had reentered the barn, returned with a long, leather switch. Leonid swished it through the air a few times, getting its feel.

"What was that all about?" Jake asked Gregarov's major domo.

"Oh, she's very new," Leonid replied. "She's an American. When she heard you speak in English, she probably thought that, being the good old American that you are, you would rescue her."

Jake palled at the thought that his mistake was going to cost this imprisoned and degraded young female a world of pain. "I'm sorry, I...." he began to say.

"Oh, don't worry," Leonid interrupted as he stepped over to the upside down, blond haired ponygirl. "It's probably better that she get this out of her system right away. She'll learn a good lesson today. She thinks that she is still a human being, when that's not true at all. The day she was outfitted with a bridle and a hood that was all over."

The tall, thin man drew the switch back and let it fly against the inner thigh of the struggling, pleading ponygirl. Jake quailed as he heard the horrific snap of the long leather whip against her flesh and her anguished cry which followed. The bit in her mouth stifled words but not sounds and the poor girl's reaction was extreme.

The blow had struck the blond ponygirl on the inner part of her right thigh, just above her vulnerable and exposed pudendum. Her body shivered and shook in response. The next blow stuck the identical location on her left thigh. The girl screamed again and made piteous pleading sounds. There were now two matching red lines of damaged flesh on her thighs. The men, Gregarov, Irkut and Jake were gathered in a kind of semi-circle around her. The grooms were standing by, enjoying the spectacle and

other hard looking men came drifting over to see what all
the fun was about.

Leonid paused to let the hot lacerations of the pony's
flesh cool and the pain subside. An effective whipping
made the ponygirl feel each painful kiss of the whip. And
waiting for the next tortuous kiss of her flesh increased the
ponygirl's anxiety dramatically.

Jake looked over at the two ponygirls that he had
agreed to buy. The two year old brunette was standing as
still as a statue. Her muscles were tense and he could see
goose bumps of fear on her large, inviting breasts. But she
was stoically holding her place. She was well disciplined.

The other ponygirl, the yearling, was not so insouciant
about the present events. He could see her body shaking
with fear. Her breasts quivered and she looked like her
knees were sagging underneath her. Although she was
looking straight ahead, away from the scene of her sister
pony's torture, Jake could sense the turmoil she was
experiencing at the sounds of the other pony's sufferings.
He wouldn't have been surprised if she feinted dead away.
After all, she was fairly new herself and may have had
fantasies of throwing herself on the mercy of one of the
many men who had undoubtedly used her body, begging
them to save her, let her go. Only time would erase that
dream. Time, training and pain.

Leonid was ready with his third stroke. Leaning over
slightly, he slashed the switch across the ponygirl's breasts.
She had apparently seen the blow coming through the tiny
outlets in her tight fitting, red hood and she had tried to
pull her chest back and away from the blow. But it came
too hard and too fast for her to deflect it. Her howl came
right after the sickening sound of a whip against flesh.
"Ooooooooooo! Ooooooooooooo!" she called out in agony.
Jake saw the plump breasts depress where the lash had
struck them. A bright red line appeared. Leonid sliced the

whip across the poor young female's defenseless mounds three more time in rapid succession. Her body jerked and spasmed as her breasts suffered the cruel blows. "Oooooooooooooo!" she cried. "Oooooooooooo!"

Some of the men who had gathered were laughing in amusement at the female's anguished contortions. By the way they were looking at her sweaty but deliciously curvaceous body, Jake assumed that she would be in for a good workout once her punishment was over. His own cock was as hard as steel. This was the first actual beating of a ponygirl he had witnessed. He had seen ponies suffer a crack or two with a whip or a riding crop, but had never been present when a determined, universal, full scale assault had been launched. It brought home like never before the fact of the unlimited freedom that the owners of these former persons had to abuse or dispose of them. Leonid could literally whip this female to death and there would be no consequences. Only her worth as an article of pleasure and amusement militated against it.

Leonid began to work the blows from the whip up the pony's body. He laid four quick, hard strokes across her taut belly above and below the fierce looking dragon that was tattooed there. She was crying and moaning now in a steady stream. More lashes were administered to the inside and outside of her thighs. After letting the miserable female settle down to a low moan, Leonid reached back over his head and delivered a vicious blow directly along the line of the pony's delicate slit. Her body seemed to contract in a painful cringe and she cried out even louder than before.

Leonid stood back from the scene of his carnage. The blond haired ponygirl was blubbering and moaning. Her body swung slowly to and fro. The top of her hood was wet with tears that had flowed down over her head. Her wide lips worked piteously against her bit. After a few moments, Leonid signaled the grooms to let the ponygirl down. She collapsed into a pile as first her head and then her torso struck the dirt beneath her. She may have assumed that her torment was at an end, but she would have been wrong. The two grooms exchanged the ropes that led to her ankles and threw them again over the top of the brackets attached to the barn. The blonde gave out a dismal moan as she felt her legs being elevated again by the ropes affixed to her black booted ankles.

When her head was again two feet off of the ground, Leonid went to work on the back of her body. He laid blows along the inside and backs of her thighs, her imprisoned arms, across her pale white rump and her lower back. Red stripes jumped out of her skin everywhere the lash touched. She wailed and cried forlornly. Finally, Leonid repeated his sadistic cruelty by giving one last stroke, this time from the back, centered on the puffed up, raw lips of her vagina. But this time the blow barely registered with Leonid's victim. She just gave out a low moan as her body absorbed it.

The men around Leonid gave him a respectful round of applause. They had witnessed a performance of a master. Jake dutifully joined in.

"What do you think of that my Yankee friend," Irkut said to Jake, slapping him on the back. "Not something you get to see every day, eh?"

"Hardly," Jake responded. Although his enthusiasm was feigned, Jake could not gainsay the stiffness of his prick and the hot lust that the beating of the ponygirl had fueled. Her body was still twitching. He wondered how the sophisticated, modern psyche of the young American girl could deal with the travail that she had just endured. She was so new to her bridle that he could see the tan lines of her bikini on her now red striped behind.

He felt another hard slap on his shoulder. This time it was Gregarov. "Let's finish our business. I've got a big party tonight. You're staying, of course?"

It was really not a question, but more of a declaration. Jake was already determined to stay. He had just witnessed graphically what Burnham's young niece had undoubtedly suffered in one form or another. His determination to find and rescue her had been dramatically reinforced. He wondered how many times she had felt the burning kiss of a lash wielded in anger. What would her mind be like now? What was the mind of any of the ponygirls like? The two year old, for example; what kept her mind going and not collapsing inwards into some form of mental black hole? Could people adjust to anything? How strong was the desire to live, after all?

Leonid attached leashes to the bits of the two ponygirls that Jake and Irkut had approved. He began to lead them up to the house. There was a large circle of sweat under each of his arms, although his face was a picture of tranquility. Jake and Irkut followed with Gregarov taking up the rear. When they reached the house, Leonid bent the ponygirls over a railing there and tied their ankles to posts. Their bits were tied off to a ring in the ground. Gregarov ran his hands over their prominent rears and patted them. "Good ponyflesh here," he said. "You won't be sorry."

Jake had performed this ritual six times before. It was getting easier and easier to do. Before recently, he had never fucked a woman in front of another man. He had had a few threesomes, but that was not the same and all of the body parts but his were female. Since there were two ponygirls to claim, Irkut would help out. He saw the older man stand between the outspread legs of the two year old brunette and begin to finger her exposed pussy from behind. Somewhat timidly, but not by all means reluctantly, Jake did the same to the black haired yearling. His cock felt as if it was ready to explode and he prayed that he would not dribble before he shot. He knew that the mere touch of the ponygirl's warm, intimate flesh on his cock would set him off. He decided that he would get her good and hot before he rammed his piece home.

He placed his hand on the proffered sex of the ponygirl and began to stroke its length. The female stiffened and mewed as he manhandled her. It was not long before her slit began to cream and her labia soften. He saw the body of the ponygirl stir as the effects of his attentions to her hot sheath began to drive her lust. He looked up and heard Irkut sigh as he plunged his piece into the moist hole of the brunette. She was bucking and moaning and he could see her muscles contract as she tried to squeeze her legs around the thick, hard rod that had invaded her.

Jake was burning with lust. The black haired yearling's pussy was hot and distended as a result of his efforts. He teased the little bud that lay atop the female's sex and heard the yearling sigh with desire. With his other hand he unleashed his prick and took it in hand. He thought of ice cream, taxes, baseball, anything but the vision of young female flesh that was bent over before him. He bit his tongue in an effort to delay the inevitable. He wanted the ponygirl to be just so hot that she would come at the moment that he penetrated her. Her hips were bucking and she was moaning with need. "Auggggg! Augggggg!" she called out. At that moment, Jake presented his cock's helmeted head to her dripping channel. With one hard push of his hips he pressed it beyond the soft folds of the female's nether lips and into the steamy hot warmth of her womb. He felt his balls tighten and his juices rise as the young ponygirl shuddered with pleasure. "Auuuuuug! Auuuuuuuuug!" she cried, her voice distorted by the cruel bit between her teeth.

The effect of the slick, constricted tunnel on his tool was too much for Jake. His needy prick exploded and he poured a thick, steady stream of his hot seed into the moaning ponygirl's cunt. Feeling his release and the heat of his discharge, the ponygirl exploded too. Her whole body shivered and shook as wave after wave of delight pored through her. Jake could feel her pussy's hard contractions around his pulsing sword. He pulled the ponygirl close to him by her hips and pushed his cock as deep as it would go. His mind was befogged with strong jolts of pleasure as he emptied himself into her.

When he again became conscious of his surroundings, Jake felt the eyes of the other men boring into him. Irkut was buttoning his fly. "Good timing Mr. Barnes," Leonid said humorously. In spite of himself, Jake smiled.

CHAPTER THREE
THE LIFE OF A RACING PONY

200 kilometers from where Jake stood, a sturdy but curvaceous young ponygirl named Lightning, formerly known as Madeline, was kneeling in a grass covered field. Her head was bent down before her, almost touching the ground. Her thighs were spread wide and her naked breasts were pressed down against the tops of her bare thighs. She was wearing the blue neoprene hood that was standard issue on the estate of Axmail Grobgy, a former NKVD operative who had taken control of a large piece of the drug and contraband trade in the Russian Republic since the dissolution of the Soviet Union. Maddy's wrists were joined behind her back, something she had gotten quite used to since they had been that way for the better part of three months. She was wearing a leather shield over the lower half of her face that covered a thick leather plug inside her mouth. She preferred the leather plug to the harsh leather covered steel bit that she wore when racing or training which pulled back on the edges of her mouth and had a sharp steel plate attached that depressed her tongue.

Maddy's vision was limited to what she could perceive peering out of the dime sized openings in the hood. Since her head was pointed downwards to the grass and there was nothing much to see there anyway, she was keeping her eyelids closed. It seemed to heighten her other senses to do so and her body tingled with the soft breeze as it ran across her skin that had been heated by the strong afternoon sun. Maddy could hear the activities of the ponygirl camp around her. The vans were being loaded and the provisions and equipment being packed. Maddy had run her tenth race in three weeks earlier that day. Things had not gone as well as planned and she and her sister ponygirl and cartmate, Persephone, were being punished.

It was not just that they had lost the race. Although they had been winners in five of their last six races, this was their second loss in a row and had been caused by what amounted to utter incompetence. It was really Maddy's fault. She had lost her footing at the start and had dragged her teammate down with her as she fell. By the time Maddy and Persephone had gotten back to their feet, the other yearling team, pulling a lightweight pony cart just like theirs, had gotten fifty or sixty meters ahead of them. It was a shame too because the green and yellow outfitted team was really no match for Maddy and Persephone, who wore the blue and gold colors of their estate. They almost closed to victory in spite of the mishap at the start, finishing only five meters behind their competitors.

Vadim, their driver and racing trainer, was livid when they returned to the pony encampment after the race. Normally, he never touched them with a whip other than to give them encouragement during a race to smarten their pace or to give a last, intense burst of speed near the end. But this time he had shackled their slave collars to rings in posts mounted in the middle of the campground and beat them savagely with a riding crop. The two ponies which were kneeling side by side in the short cut grass, bore the evidence of their travail in the deep purple and black wounds that covered their breasts, rumps and arms. No good trainer would beat a valuable ponygirl on her legs with a riding crop during racing season. It would be counterproductive.

All that afternoon, Maddy and Persephone had been left mounted on a rail, their sexes and rears available to whomsoever were pleased to use them. Now, the two naked, blue headed ponies knelt abjectly in the grass, waiting to be loaded into the van for the overnight trip to their next destination. They had no idea where they would be going since ponygirls didn't need to have such information. In fact, Maddy didn't even know where she was, not even the name of the country she was in. She didn't know Persephone's real name and had never seen her face. She had not uttered a single spoken word to anyone since she had been kidnapped many weeks ago. And, except for short, curt commands, no one spoke to her, not even to explain to her the meaning of what she knew to be her new name, '*Molnya*' in Russian, although it was tattooed in Cyrillic letters, '*молния*', across her chest.

Maddy tried to keep her mind empty as she knelt waiting to be given permission to stand and being allowed to stretch her aching legs and back. She could feel the remnants of many men's discharge leaking from her sex and rear. She had been liberally greased up before being mounted to the rail and so there was no real damage to her tender membranes. But the humiliation of being so severely used after the relative placidity of being in Vadim's care was heartbreaking, so quickly had she gone from what was an almost idyllic existence to purgatory.

The young ponygirl heard and felt footsteps of a booted man approach her. A single word command was given, one of the few words of Russian that she had been taught, and Maddy struggled to her feet. It was the voice of Vadim. He was a yellow bearded, middle aged man with short blond hair. He was a few inches shorter than Maddy, with a small build ideal for his profession of ponygirl rider. He had strong hands and wrists from many years of handling the reins of ponygirl teams. He was agile and had quick reflexes. He had ridden many a champion team and had high hopes for Maddy and Persephone. He had been enraged at the amateurish way they had lost the last race and was determined that it not happen again. Now, however, punishment time was over and it was time to reestablish the bond between himself and his racing ponies. He stood before the two contrite ponygirls and rubbed their breasts and stroked their bellies. He made soft cooing sounds to them and softened his eyes. Maddy was happy to see that she had been forgiven. Tears welled up in her concealed eyes and her throat constricted. She would do better; she would make Vadim happy and proud.

Vadim signaled the ponygirls to follow him and he led them over to the traveling van. His little blond slave girl had already rolled up the blue and gold silken panels that usually concealed the area around the van from prying eyes. She was waiting by the van for her hooded and bound charges and gave them a refreshing shower from the hose attached to the van's water tank. It was not the full, warm, luxurious shower that they usually received from her, one marked by tender caresses and soothing hands. But it was good to get the dust of the racing track off of their bodies and have the cum of multiple, unknown men washed from their loins and rears.

Once washed and fed, the ponies were led to the back of the van where they were mounted in traveling position. The rear of the van was open at the back to allow for air circulation and had a rail across its middle. The ponies were stood up with the rail pressed against their bellies. A leash fastened their collars to the front of the van and their waists were cinched to the rail. Their high, black, leather boots were attached to rings in the floor. Since they would be traveling at night, there was no need for keeping the back open to mitigate the effects of the scorching Kalikastan sun, and so a thick tarp was lowered over the back reducing the interior of the pony van to darkness. The tarp would keep the ponygirls' body heat in against the cool nighttime air of the steppes.

The drive took many hours. The rough roads kept the van rocking and jerking for most of the time. It was comforting for Maddy to be able to rub up against the thigh and arm of her cart mate during the trip. She had spent the last month or so in tandem with the other young ponygirl and had grown attached to her. It had broken her heart to see her suffer the rain of blows administered by their driver all because of her own stupid mistake. She had grown to love the other ponygirl. Vadim often let them kiss and caress each other to orgasm with their mouths, or just lay naked and intertwined, whiling the time away between training, racing and traveling.

The van arrived at its destination after a five hour trip. It was only 150 kilometers as the crow flies, but the slow pace necessitated by the poor roads made the trip much longer. It was dark outside when Maddy and Persephone were removed from the pony van and, after being allowed to pee and given long, cool drinks of water, were laid back down inside it on two inch thick cotton pallets to sleep. The ponies slept on their backs, their ankles and thighs strapped tightly together. Their boots were removed and their collars and ankles were fastened by chains to rings in the floor. There were rectangular panels on their hoods just above their eyelets held in place by a Velcro tab. At night, and sometimes during the day, these panels were lowered over the eyelets and held down by Velcro on the other side of the tabs. This shut out all light from the eyes of the ponygirl, encapsulating her in her own private sensations.

Alone, isolated, shut off from the world, it was during the minutes or sometimes hours while Maddy waited for sleep to claim her that she would begin to pine for her former life. She would struggle at her bonds and cry, ruing her cruel fate. She could often hear Persephone going through the same turmoil, shaking and moaning next to her. There was something about the night that brought the unwanted memories back. They were unwanted because they only brought misery and fear. While active during the day, Maddy was able to drive away her desperate unhappiness at having been reduced to the status of a dehumanized beast. During the active portions of the day, she was able to forget that she had been deprived of her voice and the use of her now vestigial hands. But at night, her bound arms lay beneath her and she could not ignore their existence. And in the lonely, black nights she yearned to call out from her leather filled mouth to beg God or whoever could hear her for respite from the awful nightmare she was living.

This night, Maddy lay awake for some time. For a while after she had been laid to bed she could hear the sighs and moans of the little blond slave girl through the wall of the pony van as she was ploughed by the thick, hard cock of their driver. Only a thin wall separated the pony van from the traveling van and the bed inside the traveling van was set in its rear. Maddy could hear Vadim's loud, familiar grunts as he took his pleasure. He had never fucked either of his racing ponies, but he usually allowed one of them each evening, when training and dinner were done, to suck his cock to completion, so Maddy was well acquainted with his sounds of sexual pleasure.

Maddy looked forward to taking his hot meat in her mouth. Sucking a cock was the only form of expression open to the dehumanized female. Only by giving her driver a long, tender, artful treat with her mouth could Maddy communicate her gratitude for the driver's kind treatment of her. And for the other men who used her mouth, it was the only time that she could feel that she held them in thrall, had command of the sexual act she was performing, had any individuality or will. And, oddly, she had come to relish the feel of a hard, thick penis between her lips, to enjoy the salty taste of the hardened member, the bittersweet taste of its cum. Her heart would often actually palpitate as she felt the rod of flesh throb inside her mouth or throat and feel the hot, white, creamy discharge flow into her.

When the moans and cries of the fornicating couple on the other side of the van wall subsided, Maddy's mind began to drift. She recalled her former almost carefree life, a life that seemed almost frivolous now. She remembered that awful night that she was captured, her last breath of free air. She recalled the ordeal of the slave center where she had been first shaven and adorned with the accouterments of her new life. The face of her owner loomed before her. She did not know his name but she would never forget his face. He had peered leeringly into her eyes behind her hood as he took her and drove her to her pleasure at her arrival at his vast estate, her first use as a pony girl.

She would also never forget the face of her first trainer, the man known to others as Anton Drabik, the former red Army colonel, now a professional assassin and ponygirl trainer for Grobgy's criminal empire. He had abused her unmercifully, pushed her beyond her endurance, used her callously. Yet she had come to yearn for his touch, welcome the pulse and discharge of his hard, thick prick inside her. And she would never be able to forget the way he trained her to receive pleasure through her rear, narrower passage, barring the use of her other orifices until she learned to come with only a rigid tool in her bowels.

But Drabik had abandoned her, first to a hard, cruel, blond youth who had broken her to her traces and taught her how to pull a ponycart, and then to Vadim, who had taken her over as her official driver. As she tried to find a mental formula for sleep, she wondered when her stint as a racing pony would come to an end. She knew it could not last forever. How many more races would she run before she found herself back in the pony barn subject to the random use and abuse of any male who desired her? For while she was under Vadim's tutelage, she was barred from use by anyone else. Today had been the exception. And once, after her first race, her owner had taken his right to plough her rear entrance as a reward to himself for her first racing victory. It had been a while since she had felt a hot shaft inside her intent on her pleasure and her owner's determined and forceful thrusts into her bowels had driven her to a blinding ecstasy. Otherwise, her pleasures had been confined to the deft and gentle lips and hands of Vadim's slave girl, her lustful bouts with Persephone and the hot tongue of Vadim as he licked her to orgasm at the end of each training day.

It was the thought of the sweetness of her driver's tongue that allowed sleep finally to overcome her. She slept dreamlessly for what seemed like many hours. She was awoken by the gentle hands of the slave girl as she opened the tabs to her hood and loosened the straps and chains that had kept her confined during the night.

It was a fine, brisk morning. Little puffs of soft, white clouds drifted slowly across a light blue ceiling. The sun was halfway up the sky already and the dew had been burned off of the grass. Maddy recognized instantly that they were back on the Grobgy estate, her home. She shuddered at the possibility that the racing season was over, but the kind attention she received from the little slave girl soon comforted her. The bright blue and gold panels had already been set and Maddy was able to kneel on her haunches and enjoy the cool, clean air in relative privacy.

Persephone was brought to an area next to Maddy and separated from her by one of the five foot high panels. The panels were affixed to sharp wooden posts that were stuck into the ground. The effect was as if the women were surrounded by a blue and gold corral that fluttered in the gentle breeze. A temporary panel was set up so that the slave girl could wash and feed the ponies out of sight of each other. It would not do for the ponygirls to see each other's faces. No human expression was permitted a ponygirl, not a smile, not a tender look. They were as anonymous to each other as they were to the world around them. For all Maddy knew, Persephone could be American, French, Italian, Greek, Israeli or anything else.

Maddy was attended to by the pretty little slave girl first. The diminutive, naked, young woman, wearing her leather shield gag over the lower half of her face and tight bands of leather over her wrists and ankles, gently removed Maddy's hood. Kneeling behind the pony, so that she would not see its face, the slave girl tenderly stroked Maddy's head and shoulders, comforting her. She presented Maddy with a bowl of oatmeal mixed with honey, a treat Maddy enjoyed every morning. It was a wonderful change after the almost tasteless gruel of the pony barn. After the slave girl affixed her collar to a chain that led to a post hammered into the ground, she went to feed Persephone. Maddy leaned over and, using only her mouth and tongue, slowly ingested the delicious mixture, licking the bowl clean. The bowl was ceramic, depriving the pony girl of the vision of herself that she might get from a steel one. She hardly remembered what she looked like. The slave girl had swung a blue and gold panel closed so that Maddy was in a little corral of her own, shut off from the world and yet free to enjoy the clean, fresh air and the warming sun.

After about ten minutes, the slave girl returned. Maddy had finished with the breakfast and she was given a long, cool drink of water to wash it down. The slave girl had a bowl of steaming hot water and she used it to lather a bar of soft, creamy soap to wash Maddy's pale, white face while she knelt behind her. Maddy enjoyed the sensation of the soft hands of the girl on her skin. Her ritual shaving was next, and the slave girl, after lathering Maddy's head with hot, steamy soap, drew the finely honed straight razor across it. A moisturizing cream was softly rubbed into Maddy's face and head so as to keep the skin soft and smooth to the touch. Next was the washing of her long, brown ponytail. The slave girl shampooed and dried it and combed out all of the knots.

Maddy always dreaded the reapplication of the stretchy, blue hood. For a brief period of time every morning she was able to think of herself as human, a woman, an individual. As soon as her ponytail was threaded through the hole at the back and the soft, blue fabric pulled across her face, her fantasy would be over. She was not a woman, she was a ponygirl. It only needed the reinsertion of the thick, leather gag with its mouth and chin concealing shield to complete her resumption of bestial status.

Every day, once Maddy had been reoutfitted with the impedimenta of her servitude, the slave girl would lather and shave her sex and lower stomach. Maddy would lie back, her legs spread wide, her knees raised and the slave girl would carefully draw the sharp razor over her nether lips, over her loins, scraping away all evidence of Maddy's maturity that had reestablished itself over the last 24 hours.

Maddy had gotten used to the fact of her complete nudity and the fact that her body was exposed for all to see. She wore the bright yellow tattoo of a rampant wolf on her belly, evidence of her pedigree as a ponygirl trained at Grogby's estate. She had a golden ring threaded through her nose and bright blue letters emblazoned across her chest. Her plump and firm breasts, with their dark, almost maroon areolas, stood out invitingly. It was the shaving of her pubic beard and the hairless state of her sex that shamed her. It reduced her body to a prepubescent state, yet, at the same time, it advertised her as available to all. She knew that eyes were drawn to the delicate, plump lips that framed the entrance to her womb and to the bright golden disks that were suspended from them. Her legs, arms and underarms had been permanently depilitated. They could have done that to her head and sex as well. But the ritual daily surrender of her growth to the razor drummed into her every day that her body was not her own to control. She was property, with no more rights than a cow or a dog, trimmed and groomed to her owner's pleasure.

The naked, blond slave girl dragged the sharp edged blade along the soft skin surrounding Maddy's plump mons. Her hands were soft and gentle. She knelt between Maddy's uplifted knees and slowly and carefully removed the tiny stubble that had grown there since the previous morning. Maddy stared at the light blue sky through the tiny holes in her hood silently urging the girl to completion of this humiliating ordeal. Inevitably, Maddy's slit began to moisten. Every day since her conversion to a ponygirl she had endured this ritualistic function and, every day, when the task was completed, the stable boy or the groom or her trainer, if he had deigned to perform the task himself, fingered or licked her to orgasm when they were through, sometimes finishing the job by inserting their stiff members inside her and achieving their own release. Today, when the slave girl was finished, she would massage and stroke Maddy's proffered pussy until she jerked and moaned with pleasure. Maddy's body knew it and the simple act of spreading her legs in docile cooperation with the denuding of her sex brought on an anticipatory lust.

When the slave girl finally put down the razor, Maddy's loins began to burn. She jumped slightly when she felt the tiny fingers softly stroke the length of her widening crevasse. The slave girl's touch was wholly unlike the heavy handed groping of the stable boys and grooms who thrust their thick, knowledgeable fingers between her lower lips.

The slave girl's touch was deft and light and built up in Maddy a delightful, slowly growing lust. She felt the slave girl's finger tease her nub of pleasure and a wave of tingling, electrified sensations flowed though her. A small finger breeched the tiny brown star between her rear cheeks and the tight ring of flesh there clamped down on it in a trained, automatic reaction. The supine pony girl's breath became heavy and her thighs began to tremble as the slave girl's fingers danced tantalizingly along her blood filled lower lips.

The dual agitation of Maddy's lower entrances soon had her panting with need. A long, deep moan escaped her lips and she dug her heels hard into the soft grass beneath them. Her toes curled and her body began to shake. She called out, "Ughhhh! Ughhhh!" through her gag as the first spasms pulled her pussy tight. "Ughhhhhhh! Ughhhhhh!" she cried as the jolts of her orgasm tore through her body.

When the pulses of pleasure subsided, the slave girl ran her cool hands over Maddy's hot inner thighs, over her knees and down the outside. She gently pushed Maddy's legs together and pulled them out so that they lay flat on the ground. She fastened straps around Maddy's ankles and thighs immobilizing her. Then, crawling along her body, she gently caressed Maddy's head before lowering the flaps over her eyelets. As darkness enveloped her once again, Maddy saw the smiling eyes of the pleasantly beautiful young woman.

Maddy waited in the darkness while the slave girl attended to her partner. Her whole body still reverberated with the effects of her manipulation to pleasure. Echoes of the girl's deft fingers played upon her still moist and luxuriant pussy now trapped between her belted thighs. Being confined, blinded and immobile let Maddy concentrate on the pleasant state that the slave girl had induced. She let herself be carried away on a soft raft of temporary tranquility.

After about twenty minutes, she heard Persephone's grunts and moans from the other side of the partition as she too received her morning release. Contrary to the practices in other cultures, it was widely held by ponygirl and slave trainers in Kalikastan that a steady diet of sexual stimulation built up the responsiveness of the indentured females. After a while, a day without an orgasm became a day of low level torment. Despite themselves, the females became addicted to the constant sexual activity. This was just one more way of demonstrating control over the slave girls and former women and it reminded them of their duty of constant availability.

When the slave girl was finished administering Persephone's dose of pleasure, the two ponygirls were given warm showers. When dry, the slave girl attached their collars to leads at the back of the ponyvan where they would await, standing naked in the sun, the pleasure of their driver, Vadim.

* * * * * * * * * * * *

Vadim had spent the morning at the mansion owned by Maddy's owner, Axmail Grobgy. Grobgy was intensely interested in the midseason form of his racing teams. The estate fielded seven different teams during the season, the yearling pair, of course, the 1500 and 3000 meter one pony sulky, the landau, a large formal carriage pulled by nine pony girls, a troika, requiring the service of three ponies, a brougham, a four wheeled carriage with two double seats preceded by a team of four pony girls, and a six ponied cabriolet. All of the drivers were gathered. Vodka in the morning was refreshing, especially when it was served on little sliver trays by beautiful, naked slave girls. Seven drivers and four trainers were sitting on the long, black leather couches and easy chairs that populated Grobgy's reception room. Vadim had a voluptuous, pale skinned, black haired girl over his lap and was probing her dripping slit when Grobgy finally entered. He was a large, thick boned man with wavy, black hair and a full, thick, black moustache. He called out his greeting to the other men and took a large, straight backed chair and sat in front of the expectant group. Vadim reluctantly put his squirming whore aside and directed his attention to Grobgy, his employer.

"Well," Grobgy said, his voice deep and throaty. To many a man it had been the last thing they heard before a bullet pierced their brain for some real or imagined slight. No one fucked with Axmail Grobgy. "Not bad so far," he continued. "I understand that we're in second place behind the Molokov estate. Better than we expected." Estate teams were rated on a point system, with so many points being awarded for each won race and weighted by type of event. The sulkies were the formula one of the ponygirl circuit and received the highest points for each win. The troika, being a kind of specialty race was rated the lowest.

"I told you that the troika would do well," one of the men said, a trainer.

"So you did," Grobgy replied. "The sulkies are holding up well too. It's the landau that worries me." He looked over at a rather nervous older man with brown hair mottled with gray and a pock marked face. He was the landau trainer. Next to him sat the also nervous driver, a tall, thin man with close cropped black hair, a longish nose and tight, thin lips. He licked them now. It was not easy to manage a nine pony team.

"We've got three days of rest here to work on them," the driver said, his voice tentative. "We need to get their timing down better. I think it's the third row. There's a couple of pretty old ponies in there."

The nine ponied landau, pulled by three rows of three ponygirls each, was usually relegated to the bigger, stronger, albeit slower, ponies. They were ponies who had lost their real racing edge but had built up strong muscles and physiques over their years of racing. They were fed special diets to maximize their bulk while keeping body fat to a minimum. But when a pony got tired and old, it was just time for them to go.

The ponies in the front two rows often pulled other racing carts as well, doubling up with the landau. But the number three row was almost always a problem, even for an estate as large as Grobgy's.

"Work them good today and tomorrow." Grobgy ordered. "And then let them rest a day. Give the third row some special treatment. That ought to get them working a little harder." Special treatment did not imply cake and candles. Landau ponies 7, 8 and 9, were in for some 'motivational sessions'.

Grobgy looked at Vadim. Lightning and Persephone's success had been a bonus for the estate team. Grobgy was concerned at the two recent losses. "And?" he asked the golden haired driver.

"They'll be okay. They blew the start at the last meeting. The race before that was a tough one. The track was wet and Persephone twisted an ankle. I'm going to be working on some fundamentals with them over the next couple of days. They'll sparkle in the second half, believe me."

Grobgy smiled at Vadim's assessment. His yearling team had gotten a late start in training, Lightning and Persephone having been acquired only in early March. Other yearling teams had been working over the winter in special winter training barns used during the cold, snowy season. National Commission rules prohibited yearling team training until after January 1, but it was a rule often honored in its breach. The Grobgy estate had no winter training barn of its own, a fact often bemoaned by Maddy's trainer, Drabik.

"Do I smell a divisional championship?" Grobgy asked, his eyes alight. "That would put us over the top for sure." Grobgy's estate had finished third in each of the last three seasons and the points that a yearling championship would garnish could just be the additional edge they might need to win the coveted Estate Cup.

"I'd say there is a very good chance," Vadim replied proudly. "The team gets stronger every day. Especially Lightning. Sometimes I think that she is just dragging Persephone along for the ride. Her reactions are, well, lightning fast. That's what caused the mishap in the last race. Lightning is so strong and quick, she leapt off the starting line and left Persephone standing still."

Grobgy's interest was peaked. Drabik had told him that there was something special about her when she was just a new pony. Maybe he was right. "Do you think that she might be sulky class?" he asked. Sulky ponies, running solo in front of a two wheeled cart and a driver were the fastest ponies in the sport. Those with both speed and endurance ran the Grand Prix of pony racing, the 3000 meter sulky race.

"Undoubtedly," Vadim said. "By fall she'll be ready to compete with the best."

That reminded Grobgy. "Pieter," he asked, "how's Starlight's leg?" Starlight ran the 1500 sulky. She had suffered a pulled calf muscle in training and had gotten off to a slow start, going 3 and 3. However, she had won her last four races and was apparently getting back to her usual form. She had won a silver in the 1500 meter divisional championship last fall. Pieter was her trainer.

"She's looking good. Jerzi's been pacing her well." Jerzi Gromyko was her four foot high driver. All the other classes had their minimum weight for drivers, but the sulky class had no limits. Those racing carts were mostly driven by men of dwarfish stature. Jerzi was a little over 4' tall. He drove the 1500 sulky and his younger brother, Giorgi drove the 3000. Giorgi was about 4'2" tall. Although small, they were both immensely strong and had no difficulty in handling the sulky reins.

"I ice it every night and have a special liniment that we use," Jerzi told Grobgy, his tiny legs hanging off of the edge of the couch. He was small, but was strong, and his dark features and angry eyes bespoke a determined form of cruelty. The Gromyko brothers were the premier sulky drivers in the sport. Objections might have been made regarding the rigorous program of torment of the ponies under their charge, but no one could argue with success. Jerzi continued. "You never can tell. There's a tough race coming up this week. Kerensky's sulkies are top notch and we race them here Saturday. I'll have to let her go all out to win."

Grobgy remained silent for a moment, musing his options. They could hold off. Starlight would definitely make the finals and would qualify for the divisional championships whether or not she won Saturday. But Kerensky had a tough stable and he might need the points at the end of the season. If they lost too many races to Kerensky on Saturday they could fall behind in the overall team championship.

"Okay," he said. "Let's go for it. She's been running good and the track looks like it will be dry. I want those points."

Jerzi and Pieter nodded in agreement. The meeting lasted another hour or so. The men discussed the other teams, the ponies that were in reserve, meaning ones that were good enough to race but not assigned to a team, the current state of the new yearlings. Drabik reported on the tall, strong Australian pony he had been training. She had good strength and speed. She had just been broken to a cart the other day and was finding it hard going. But she could be thrown into the yearling team if it came to a pinch and one of the racing yearlings was injured.

"Let her practice with Vadim's team a couple of times from both the right and the left," Grobgy ordered. Yearlings, having had less training and conditioning than the other ponies, were more prone to injury. It was always a good bet to have one in reserve.

The meeting broke up and the slave girls emerged from the shadows with a few more trays of cold shots of Vodka. Vadim took the tall, thin Irish girl he had been toying with before Grobgy came in by the collar.

"Do you mind?" he asked he black haired gangster.

"Be my guest," Grobgy replied.

* * * * * * * * * * * *

The long haired, thin, Irish girl drew her pursed lips down the length of the blond haired Russian's stiff prick as he leaned back on the large overstuffed pillows in the guest room bed. His eyes were closed, bespeaking a momentary distraction from the worries of a ponygirl racing driver. The young woman's long, delicate fingers rested softly on his widespread thighs as her straight, black hair fell around her face like a shimmering, obsidian curtain. Vadim groaned with delight as the young girl changed course, pulling her head back while twirling her dexterous tongue over the length of his shaft. The girl, swooped from the Dublin streets a mere five weeks ago, had only arrived at Grobgy's estate the day before. She had spent the better part of her captivity so far in the cellars of the rigorous training facility in the basement of a pre-revolution mansion in the outskirts of the capital. She had been deemed a quick learner and had been shipped out two days ago. Long, angry, red stripes along her back and over her firm, pointed, coffee cup sized breasts bespoke her initiation into her new duties by her new, callous master. Grobgy made it a habit to greet all of his newly acquired female property personally and a round or two with a long, leather switch usually was sufficient to drive into a new slave girl the need for enthusiasm in her fresh surroundings.

The pale skinned girl had trembled with fear as Vadim had escorted her up the winding marble staircase of the mansion. She was accoutered with the leather collar and bracelets typical of her status, and the black leather contrasted nicely with her ghostly pallor. She had waited nervously on the pale green, satin sheets of the king sized bed while Vadim had undressed himself. She had hoped and prayed that her naked slit would be moist enough for the satisfaction of this strange, hard man who had culled her out from the slave girl crowd downstairs. She had been taught well enough over the last few weeks the importance of making herself ready for use, lessons that had been costly in pain and suffering. As she knelt on the bed, her hands drawn behind her back, her knees spread, she tried to think of all the things that could maker her wet.

Kim had been a shopgirl by day and a rather wild carouser by nights. She had spread her 19 year old legs rather indiscriminately for the rough, young lads who populated the rowdy rock and roll clubs of the Irish capital. She was from out in the west, a small village that sat on the Atlantic Coast, a place full of fishermen and fishermen's wives. She had fled to the Republic's largest city as soon as she had saved up enough for a flat. She was a lithe, saucy mouthed beauty with bright green eyes and long, languorous legs. A few small drops of a soporific in her beer, a woozy stroll outside for air with a handsome lad she had just met and a brief ride in the trunk of a black limousine had been enough to place her in the stream of commerce. Her rockin' days were over, but her life could, and would, on occasion still get kind of wild.

Kim went mentally to the place where she had been taught. Her mind recalled orgasms and deep, passionate kisses. There was a boy back in Killala, the nearest thing to a city to her place of birth, who had driven her wild one night with his tongue buried deep in her tight, young hole. She drew her mind to that recollection and her slit began to obediently moisten.

Vadim, when he was finished undressing, pushed her unceremoniously to her back and crawled between her obedient, widespread legs. When he pressed the head of his already rock hard prick against Kim's dilated labia, they parted easily and he was able to slide his manhood effortlessly deep within her. The black haired girl moaned as she felt herself filled. She wrapped her arms around the slight but sturdy man and pulled his lips to hers. If she was to be fucked, she wanted to get off. By now she had been raped a hundred times and the strangeness of the man's flesh and her lack of choice in copulating with him was dismissed from her mind. She would cry later, tonight in her little slave cell, assuming that she was not wanted in her master's or anyone else's bed.

Kim wrapped her long legs around Vadim's thighs and pulled the appreciative blond man's cock deep within her. He grunted as he ploughed her crevasse, dragging his tool across her blood filled, hardened clit. She could tell that Vadim was a man who liked to fuck since he took his time with her, shifting his rhythms, slowly pulling his conscienceless rod out of her hot slit until just its helmeted head lay inside her and then easing himself back in until he was buried to the hilt.

As her lusts rose, Kim began to moan. She was thrusting her hips hard back at her assailant, her body writhing beneath him. His tongue enflamed her and her heart thumped in her chest. She came before he did, gripping him tightly, crying out into his mouth. As her orgasm tore through her, she felt the nameless man tense between her legs and his warm discharge splash within her.

Vadim had showered while the Irish slave girl waited obediently for him crouched on her hands and knees on the bed. When he had dried himself, he sat down at the head of the bed and pulled her up by the hair. He spoke one of the few Russian phrases that she knew and she quickly proceeded to take his softened manhood between her lips. And here was where we found them, her pursed lips treating Vadim's cock to the pleasure of their moist warmth. Kim tried to blank out her mind while she concentrated at her task. At least this man was clean and he had fucked her so well. As a result, she put a little more effort into it as a reward. Now she was about to receive the benefit of her labor as the well muscled, but thin man sighed and moaned, his hot cock burning her lips and mouth. "Aaaaaaarh!" Vadim groaned as his cock pulsed and throbbed, sending his cum spurting into the girl's skilled mouth. His eyes fluttered and his thighs shook as the ecstasy of his spasms jolted through him.

"Grobgy's got the best whores," he thought as the girl's energetic lips prolonged his mind blowing throbs. He placed his hands on the obedient girl's head and pushed it down, running his meat into her throat. He sent his last few spurts of creamy, white discharge down her esophagus while the girl gagged and moaned. He kept her head there until he was sure his balls had emptied themselves and his cock had calmed. He released her just as her need for air had begun to become acute.

Ten minutes later, as he walked along the path to the ponygirl campground, Vadim was physically sated but mentally unsettled. For the better part of an hour, while he had been fucking that delightful Irish girl, he had been able to push out of his mind the anger that had seized him when Grobgy had suggested trying out the Australian pony in his team. He had been hired to run a specific team and had accepted the job only after giving Lightning and Persephone a hard workout. Now, just when it appeared that he had a possible championship team in hand, it looked like Grobgy might move Lightning up to the sulky class if Starlight got hurt. He wouldn't be surprised to see her running in front of one of those small, streamlined carts over the next three days.

When he arrived at his van, he saw his ponies standing tethered dutifully at its rear. He stopped to caress their breasts and stroke their heads. They were a good team. If only he could keep them.

A half hour later, Vadim had his team out on the practice track trotting through some laps. Although the 1500 meter yearling race was about a lap and a ¼ around the track, endurance was important to speed and he liked to get the ponies a good, long workout when he could. He would run them ten laps slow and then five laps fast for a couple of hours. Then they would be showered, massaged, pleasured to climax and allowed to relax for a few hours. He would walk them around the track for a while in the early evening and then call it a day. Tomorrow, they would work on starts.

Maddy enjoyed the strain of the long distance pulls. She, of course, had no idea what her trainer had in mind when she was harnessed up, only that she would be going for a workout. There was none of the normal commotion of a racing day and they had not been outfitted in their racing colors. It was satisfying to Maddy to see the grooms and other trainers watching from the sidelines as she went through her paces with Persephone. She knew that she and her cartmate had earned their admiration. It was, though, nothing like the roar of the crowd on race day. There was something about the frantic, almost delirious reactions of the crowd that, despite her underlying unhappiness and misery at being deprived of all human qualities, made her chest swell with excitement. And when they won, she was filled with pride. Somehow, oddly, being part of a winning ponygirl team made her feel valued, special. It was something to live for.

She and Persephone were standing at rest, their heads bent over, their chests heaving, their muscles aching wonderfully after their five lap dash around the track when Maddy saw a pair of familiar boots step up in front of her. It was her trainer, Drabik. She didn't know his name, but she knew his moods and preferences intimately. She hadn't seen him for several weeks. Her stomach turned when she realized who it was. The last time she had been in his control he had treated her miserably. She knew in her heart that he was waiting for her to be returned to the pony barn. She saw his rough, hard hand reach out for her breast and seize her plump nipple. He squeezed it tightly, uttering her name in his deep, menacing voice, "*Molnya.*"

It was as if ice had begun to flow in her veins. Maddy's knees weakened and she uttered a plaintive whine. It was not the sharpness of the pressure on her thick, tender nipple. It was the fear of this man who had kept her in thrall for so many weeks, the knowledge that her relative idyll would eventually end. The fact that she had no knowledge when it would end made it all the worse.

Standing next to Drabik was the smallest, most misshapen man that Maddy had ever seen. What role this demonic looking creature would have in her life, if any, frightened her. If they would only talk to her, tell her what to expect! How long would she have to be a ponygirl? Would she ever be human again?

Maddy felt the cart behind her lighten as Vadim jumped down off of it. She heard his reedy, sharp voice.

"What the fuck are you doing?" he said to Drabik in Russian. "Get away from my pony!" He spoke harshly, angrily. Although she did not know the meaning of the words, from the tone of the voice, Maddy could sense that her fear was justified.

"Fuck yourself," Drabik retorted in words just as harsh. "This isn't your pony, remember? You're just using it."

"She's mine for the racing season. You can tell Grobgy that he can look elsewhere for an understudy for Starlight," Vadim said angrily.

"Tell him yourself, asshole," Drabik responded. "You're part of a team here, Vadim, whether you like it or not. The point is that the estate must win the championship. All other goals are secondary. And remember this, even you can be found in a ditch somewhere someday. So watch your mouth."

Coming from Drabik, this was a very real threat. Everyone knew that Drabik was Grobgy's triggerman and there were some pretty horrific stories that had made the rounds. If only half of them were true....

Vadim's tone softened. "Come on Anton," he said, trying to establish a level of familiarity with the cold hearted gangster. "You know how much work I've put into this pair. It would be a shame to break them up. And what makes you think that Lightning would be ready for a sulky. She's only had three months or so of training. Some of those other ponies have been at it for years. They're hard and lean. What's the difference if Lightning or some other pony loses the 1500 sulky if Starlight gets hurt? A yearling championship would mean a lot of points. And there's a good chance that this team can win it. I know.

I've driven a dozen yearling teams. These ponies have what it takes. You'd be taking a good team and making two bad ones."

Drabik, not wanting to make Vadim shit his pants, took a conciliatory tone. "Look, it might never happen. Starlight's been running well. But we need a backup plan. We just want to watch her run."

The dwarf had been silent during the argument between Drabik and Vadim. Why jump in when Vadim had no real say in the matter. Besides, he had his doubts too. Vadim was a pussy where ponies were concerned. It would take a lot to whip this coddled pony into sulky shape. In his experience, sulky ponies had to virtually fear for their lives before they'd run the way they needed. You didn't get that by softstroking them.

Taking advantage of the lull in the argument and Vadim's obvious recognition of his limited say in what happened to the pony, Jerzi took the opportunity to give her a private inspection. The two other men looked on as he ran his two hands down each of Maddy's legs, felt her haunches. Maddy was, to say the least, disconcerted at this manhandling of her. Whatever argument the men had been having, she sensed that her driver had lost. The repulsive little man grabbed her nether lips and squeezed them, watching for the pony's reaction. Her obvious discomfiture amused him. You would think that they would get used to it. But they never did.

Even Persephone was disturbed at the unfathomable activity between the men. She was not in as good a position as Maddy to see what was going on since her bit was restrained tightly by the lead than ran directly to the cart. As any good driver would, Vadim had tied them off firmly when he descended the cart. Persephone could not move her head side to side without an immediate and discouraging pain from the metal plate in her mouth. She stared straight ahead through her tiny eyeholes in her hood. But she knew enough from the tone of the men's discussions to be skittish and afraid. For ponygirls, change was usually a bad thing. And the former UCLA art student had come to care for her pony counterpart. Like Maddy, she didn't know who her cartmate was really, where she came from, what her real name was, but she had come to know her moods and foibles well and enjoyed her companion's dexterity with her tongue.

Jerzi gave the order to kneel and the two ponies compliantly lowered themselves. Now Jerzi could inspect Maddy's broad shoulders and neck, the heart of a ponygirl. A pony could be as fast as the wind, but if it didn't have the strength to pull a ponycart, it was useless. He pinched and prodded Lightning's shoulders and back. Standing behind her, after stepping over the long, shiny, hardwood pole connected to Lightning's hip, he reached around her chest and grabbed her breasts. "Fine, full breasts," he thought. "I'll enjoy playing with these. If not this year then the next."

The diminutive pony driver stepped out from between the yokes and pronounced Lightning a good specimen. "She's got what it takes physically," he announced. "I need to see how she runs. I'll take her out after lunch." All was decided.

"You can run the Australian," Drabik told Vadim. "Get a feel for her in case worse comes to worse."

And so, after lunch, Maddy found herself strapped into the harness of a sulky pony. She had wept inside as the leather braces were applied by the cruel looking dwarf as she knelt in the dust. The sulky cart was somewhat heavier than the one half load of the cart that Maddy was used to pulling. Jerzi took her slowly around the track a couple of times. Vadim had his yearling cart out too and Maddy recognized her cartmate running next to a tall, lanky pony

she had never seen before. She just caught glimpses of
them from the eyelets in her hooded head, but what she
saw made her disconsolate.

After the third lap, Jerzi pulled Lightning to a halt near
the starting line. He hopped down from the cart and came
to stand in front of the sweating pony. He had a three foot
long quirt in his hand. Standing back and without
comment, he gave Lightning five sharp lashes with the
leather whip. Lightning hopped and squealed as the lash
ripped across her breasts, her stomach, her thighs. "What
have I done?" she thought miserably. But she had done
nothing. And when the small man showed her the whip
when he was finished, Lightning's skin burning from its
abuse, the unhappy pony realized the message. This was a
sample of what she would suffer if she failed to do her best.
She rubbed her booted feet on the track nervously and
uttered a little, high pitched, fearful grunt in
understanding, accented by a small nod of her confined
head.

Jerzi jumped up back into the lightweight cart and
snapped the reins once. Lightning jumped off instantly.
He hadn't signaled a sprint and, as her training taught her,
Lightning trotted slowly ahead. After about fifty meters,
the reins snapped again, twice sharply. This was the signal
to run and Lightning sprang into action. She dug the toes
of her heavy, black boots deeply into the soft, brown turf
and pumped her legs furiously. The sulky cart jumped after
her. She felt the whip stinging her backside and shoulders
again and again. Fearfully, Lightning poured all of her
strength into her chore. This was not like the almost
companionable teamwork of her other cart. This was work!

After about another fifty meters, Jerzi gave the signal to
slow down, a single pull back on the reins. But he didn't
use the deft, almost gentle touch that Vadim used. It was a
single, hard pull that pinched Lightning's tongue painfully

and brought a wave of nausea to her. Alarmed by the dwarf's cruel technique, Lightning slowed immediately. Her chest was heaving and her heart beating wildly. She gave an inward cry. "Is this my new life?" she thought. He heart sank at the prospect.

Fifty meters slow were followed by another fifty meters fast. Lightning had never heard of interval training, designed to increase endurance and to develop quick accelerations, but it was a technique that Jerzi and his brother Giorgi swore by. That it took a heavy mental toll on the ponies was of no concern to them.

Jerzi drove Lightning three times around the track at fifty meter intervals. Lightning's legs ached and her back and shoulders were sore from the strain. Somehow, when she was finally allowed to rest, she knew that they were not finished. And she was right. Jerzi let Lightning rest as long as it took him to smoke one of the thick, unfiltered, Russian cigarettes he liked, the ones with finely cut, black tobacco. Lightning could smell the heavy scent of the cigarette and sensed that her rest spell would last as long as it did. Her throat was parched and she yearned for a drink of water. But Jerzi wanted to see what the three month old pony could do under stress.

Lightning felt her reins snap once and she instantly began trotting ahead. When they came to the starting line, Jerzi brought her to a halt. He descended from the sulky cart once more and berated Lightning with the small whip again. Lightning winced and squirmed at the pain, moaning and begging for mercy from behind her gag. Jerzi smiled at her when finished. The red stripes from the whip stood out nicely on the pony's pale, white flesh.

The fiendish man didn't have to tell Lightning that this was her real test. Recovering from her assault, she waited for the oral signal to dig in and prepare to race. Ponygirls were not permitted to anticipate orders or do anything on

their own. She was sure that this went double for the
small, hard man who was driving her. When she heard the
Russian word for 'ready', the anxious ponygirl dug her toes
deeply into the track. There were a few moments of quiet
pause. Men had gathered at the fence to watch a master at
work. Jerzi nodded to the timekeeper who stood sentry at
the staring post, roared a command and Lightning took off.

The naked, blue headed pony leaned forward into her
task. She grunted loudly in self encouragement. Her large
breasts flung themselves wildly around on her chest. Her
legs and shoulders were tired, but all that seemed to go
away as soon as she had gotten three steps into the sprint.
She could hear her driver calling out to her as she sped
down the track. 1500 meters is a little under a mile and a
good ponygirl pulling a sulky cart could do it in about seven
and a quarter minutes. Jerzi had a good sense of time and
he was startled at how well Lightning did at the quarter
post. He laid the whip into her shoulders nonetheless,
urging her onwards. Lightning grunted at each sharp crack
of the whip on her body and dug deeper and stronger into
the turf. At the half mile, Lightning was well under a good
time. At three quarters she was just over five minutes,
thirty seconds. As the finish loomed ahead of her,
Lightning felt the whip bite harder and harder into her
back. She yearned for the finish line, craved it and she
reached down into her soul and found a huge reserve of
strength. Faster and faster she ran, causing the little
ponycart to jump along the turf. She could hear the dwarf
yelling louder and louder, cracking his whip time and time
again. And finally, she was across. She felt the painful pull
on her reins and, despite its intense discomfort, welcomed
it. Jerzi slowed the pony to a trot and brought her around
the track one more time to give her muscles a chance to
cool down. When they reached the finish line again, he

pulled the pony to a halt and jumped down in excited anticipation.

The time keeper was waving the stopwatch at him. "Six minutes, fifty five seconds!" he burst out.

CHAPTER FOUR
AN UNEXPECTED DELIGHT

At 6'2", 240 lbs., Michael Burnham made an imposing presence in a board room. Few had the intestinal fortitude to oppose his demands and he ran his corporate empire like a personal fiefdom. He was used to giving commands and having them assiduously carried out. But nothing in his sometimes tooth and nail fight to achieve and maintain his vast fortune had prepared him for the alacrity with which his newly acquired slave girls carried out his every whim.

He was sitting in a vast hot tub that was built into the bathroom off the master suite of his fabulously appointed mansion deep in the Kalikastan plains. A small, hot mouth, warmer than the 80 degree water, surrounded his hard, seven inch long prick. It belonged to the little blond haired slave girl that had been a gift of the National Commission when they had signed the construction contracts that would lead to a sea of fresh green, red and blue cash that would soon engulf the renegade republic. Next to her, her head bobbing expectantly above the water, knelt the brown haired whore he had acquired last week. She was awaiting her turn on his pole, which would come when the blond girl exhausted her supply of oxygen.

It had not been difficult to explain to the two English speaking wenches what he wanted. The blond headed slave, a former California surfer girl named Mandy, would signal the brunette, a former University of Alabama cheerleader named Brenda, by tapping her on the leg. She would then immerse herself and take her turn on the pole, giving Burnham an almost seamless flow of oral pleasure. Burnham was amused to watch when the head of each frantic slave girl breeched the bubbling waters, her eyes wide with fear and tension, her mouth sucking down a lungful of reinvigorating air.

Their job, as Burnham had explained it to them, was to keep him hard and pleasured, but not to cause his long, thick cock to explode into orgasm. They would kneel in between his heavy, widespread thighs and, with his organ encased in their mouths, exert just enough activity to keep a steady flow of delight echoing throughout his body, but not enough to send him over the top.

Burnham had been shocked when he had first been exposed to a world that he, despite all his connections and the vast information gathering potential of his corporate machine, had no inkling existed. He recalled whimsically his first tentative, almost bashful, command to a slave girl to suck his prick. Jake's men had kidded him about it. But he was long past that now. Now he realized that there was no other better way to live.

He watched as Brenda took a deep breath of air and disappeared beneath the churning water of the tub. A moment later, he felt a careful exchange of lips on his cock and, immediately afterwards, saw the gasping head of Mandy pop out of the water. He sighed as he felt Brenda's lips descend his pole. It was getting late and almost time for his videoconference with New York. Placing his one hand on Brenda's submerged and bobbing head, he reached for Mandy's firm, grapefruit sized breasts and, grabbing a stiff nipple, pulled her towards him. The surfer girl nestled next to him and offered her pretty, little mouth to his. Burnham sank his long, heavy tongue into her mouth and pulled her head against his face. This was the signal for the submerged slave girl to finish him off.

Brenda's tongue and mouth began to work energetically on his stiff, inflamed cock. She knew that she would not have a chance for air until Burnham had unloaded his hot, white cum into her mouth, not if she didn't want a severe whipping Mandy, feeling for her sister slave girl's plight, dutifully intermingled her tongue with her owner's and rubbed her gorgeous, tanned breasts against his chest. Burnham's body shuddered as he felt his moment approach. His balls were tight and tingled with anticipation. He grabbed the hair of the blond beauty behind her head and mashed his lips down hard against hers. With his other hand, he pressed the brown haired Brenda's head down onto his pole, causing the slave girl to writhe and struggle. Suddenly, his crisis was upon him and he felt the hot juices being pumped into the desperate mouth. "Oh!... Oh!... Oh!..." he called out in a heavy, deep voice as the jerking spasms of his manhood made his whole body tense repeatedly.

It took about twenty seconds for his load to fully discharge. He could feel the gentle pressure of Brenda's head as she urged it upwards, desperate for permission for relief. Burnham waited until he felt his manhood soften and then released his grip on the struggling brunette. He laughed to himself as her face rose above the surface of the water like a breeching sea monster. He watched her cough and gasp, her face a mask of air deprived agony.

When Brenda had achieved relative equilibrium, she opened her mouth and displayed for Burnham's benefit the oozy, pasty results of his orgasm. He nodded to the obedient girl. He had instructed them never to swallow without permission. He watched as the two shapely, nubile young women embraced, locked their delicate, appealing lips together and shared the reward for their labors. When done, they dutifully turned their heads and bowed respectfully to their master. He nodded to them and they let the salty load slide down their throats.

The video conference was uneventful. Burnham had set up a large communications room on the first floor of the mansion. There were three video screens a bank of laptops and a long, red oak conference table surrounded by fifteen maroon, cushioned chairs. Today, Burnham sat alone in the room. New York was eight hours behind Kalikastan and it was eight o'clock at night there. Burnham had dressed in a dark green running suit. He was not one to stand on the ceremony of corporate attire when he did not have to.

On the other end of the scrambled video line sat Tim O'Donnell, Burnham's executive vice president.

"Good afternoon, boss," O'Donnell said eagerly.

"Same to you," Burnham replied. "What's the closing report?"

"Burnham Limited is up 7 ½. Midcom is down ¼. It looks like we'll be ready to put Renthro Airlines in play in the next 48 hours. So far no rumors have hit the street and we should be able to take everyone by surprise. By Friday we should hold 25%. We'll make our tender offer on Monday."

"Good. Good. And what about the steel agreement with the Chinese? Did we get what we wanted?"

"Almost everything. Lin Pao, the president of Shanghai Industries, wanted a 35 cent per ton 'discount' to be contributed to his offshore account. We got him down to 10 cents. I don't think we'll be getting the volume of sales that we want since that Canadian outfit is undercutting us. But we agreed to hold the price for seven months. That was the clincher."

"Okay," Burnham replied. "You should have gotten the first $40 million wire transfer today on the pipeline contract. I've sent a coded email to explain how it should be broken up. We're using the Cayman Islands subsidiary to run this whole thing. It's a cost plus contract, believe it or not, and we should be able to work up our 'handling" fees pretty high by moving all the heavy supply contracts through there. Mark up all costs by 7% and then resell it to our local company here at another 7%. I'll handle the distribution of commissions here."

"Sure thing," O'Donnell responded. After a few moments he added. "When are you coming back to New York?"

Burnham laughed. "Maybe never. I'm going to set it up so that we can run the whole show from here. I want you and my personal staff out here next week. I've already made the arrangements with the Kalikastan government for visas. "

"You want Liz to come too?"

Liz was Burnham's personal secretary. She was a finely shaped, handsome woman, about 42. She had been with Burnham for years. She knew where plenty of bodies were buried and Burnham had always wondered how he could ever wholly ensure her discretion. Two weeks in Kalikastan would seal her lips for good while not depriving him of her invaluable assistance. He had always wondered what her gracefully full breasts looked like underneath her cultured corporate attire. Soon he would know.

"Liz too. Tell her that I'll need her for at least a month." That should be enough time to get her properly trained. Once sufficiently broken, she would write home and tell everyone that she was staying for the foreseeable future.

Burnham continued. "The Nikkei exchange opens at 3 a.m. local time. I'll call you at 4, 12 a.m. your time to go over the opening prices."

"Okay boss," O'Donnell said agreeably. "And I'll see you in person in a couple of days."

Burnham rang off the video connection. His next appointment was with a local security company. He still had Jake's men around, but the size of his local operation was growing and he needed his own private army just like all the other pirates and cutthroats he was doing business with.

The prospect of meeting with Nicholai Boradin, the head of the security team he was looking to retain, brought Jake to mind. Jake was due back the day after tomorrow. Already a few of the racing ponies he had bought had been delivered. They looked good and Burnham's trainers already had a few of them taking turns around the training track. The prior owner had left his supply of pony carriages behind when he went to meet his maker. Watching those shapely females tug their carts around the track, sweating and groaning under their burdens, had been almost surreal. He had almost creamed the first time he had caressed the breast of a mud splattered, chest heaving pony when she had finished a dash around the track. He had watched later when some of the grooms fucked her in the pony barn. She squealed and moaned just like a human female when she came.

And thinking about Jake and the pony girls brought back the reason that he was in Kalikastan in the first place: Maddy. He knew that Jake had so far been unsuccessful in his search for Maddy because they had worked out a coded response for their nightly telephone calls. Jake had found out nothing about Maddy, but he and Irkut had sent back some delightful pony flesh.

The operations in Kalikastan had been meant as a diversion for the hunt for Maddy. But it had opened a whole new world for him. What was the sense of living in the West where money and power were carefully circumscribed in what they could do? He couldn't have two pretty little whores at his beck and call like Mandy and Brenda back in the States. He could, at best, rent them, and still he would not enjoy the freedom to use and dispose of their bodies as he did here. No, he was never going back, except perhaps on occasion for business purposes.

But he still wanted to find Maddy, his only niece. He owed it to her. How he would square it with the local ruling junta when he released her from bondage he still didn't know.

* * * * * * * * * * * * * * * *

Jake was on his way to his third estate in four days. In the back seat of the SUV was the pretty slave girl he had taken a fancy to at the Gregarov Estate. He had attended the party the night of his arrival and a splendid party it was. Dozens of local 'gentry' came, the men sharply outfitted in tailor made tuxedos and the ladies in all of their finery. Most of the women were young and beautiful, although a few of the men brought along women who had obviously been with them for years. The guests had free range of the house and Jake saw a number of them climbing the wide, white marble staircase with a shapely, young slave girl in tow.

The liquor flowed freely and the food was first class: lobster and caviar, big, red marbled steaks, the freshest vegetables in delicate sauces. There was a floor show in the middle of the party consisting of an enticing dance by about a dozen naked slave girls, their duties as waitresses temporarily suspended.

Outside, the ponies for the next day's races were prominently displayed and Jake had a chance to take a close look at them. It was difficult to tell them apart, their faces all hooded. But none bore the tell tale birthmark that Maddy had on her hip.

Jake had stayed for the races the next day and he was surprised at the crowd that the event drew. The grandstands were filled with laughing, cheering people and the betting was heavy. Even Jake was carried away with the thrill of watching the teams compete. He admired the speed and enthusiasm of the one pony sulkies, but he most enjoyed the nine ponied landau race. The landau carriages were made of ornately carved wood with fine gold appointments. They were bedecked with the flags of their estates. It was amazing to watch the nine pony teams dash along the track with military precision in highly skilled coordination. Huge, silk uniformed drivers sat on the driver's box urging the teams on with long whips. Unfortunately for Jake's host, the other team won. It was thrilling to watch the green and white team take a victory lap around the track and then ease into the winner's circle to receive their victory wreaths and the congratulations of the crowd.

The races ended about five o'clock and he and Irkut had arranged for a late afternoon start for their next destination. Gregarov himself was waiting for them as their bags were loaded into the SUV. The blond haired slave girl from the little welcoming ceremony the day before was standing next to him, a leash draped from the ring in her collar to his mighty right hand.

"A present, my friend, for you," he said to Jake, smiling largely.

"Mr. Burnham will be pleased," Jake answered. He felt a pang of jealousy for his multi-millionaire boss.

"No, no!" Gregarov answered. "For you! A very nice piece. A man of substance needs a whore."

Jake was tempted to refuse. Owning a slave himself would be just one more step into depravity. This was a job, he tried to tell himself. When he was done, he was going home to Chicago, to play his sax in a blues club for a long time. He had done enough and he didn't think that he would ever be able to live with what he had done already. He had engineered the takeover of the slaving outfit back in the States. He had arranged for the crew to keep the operation going. How many young girls were now in chains because of him, he wondered. On the other hand, she was already a slave. If it wasn't him who owned her it would be somebody else. Besides, he didn't want to insult Gregarov. Word like that would get around pretty fast and might make it difficult to deal with the other gang leaders. Irkut jammed an elbow into his side.

"Mr. Gregarov is doing you an honor," he whispered to Jake. "Don't even think of refusing."

Jake stepped up to the broad shouldered bearded racketeer and took the leash from him. "I thank you Mr. Gregarov. I can't think of any way I can repay you. I'll be in your debt."

"Yes," Gregarov said a smirk on his face. "But only a little."

And so now as they rode the bumpy roads of central Kalikastan, the blond haired, naked slave girl rode quietly in the back seat. At Irkut's insistence she remained gagged and wore a black hood over her head during the trip. Slave girls were to be kept in as much ignorance as to their fate as possible. From time to time, Jake looked back to watch her. Her arms were pinned to her sides by a leather belt and the black hood she wore made her seem like a mystery guest. She had fine, billowing breasts and they swayed gently as the car maneuvered over the rough road. He name was stenciled over her chest in blue, Cyrillic letters and she wore the tattoo of her former owner, the angry, yellow dragon on a field of blue, etched into her lower belly. Jake remembered her frightened face as she was led into the car and was strapped into the seat. The saucer like blue eyes looked at the world pleadingly as the black hood was lowered over them. There was a slight mewing sound from behind her gag. Since then she had been silent.

They drove until just after nightfall, around eight P.M. It would not due to put the Range Rover in a huge pothole. Irkut directed the SUV into the parking lot of an inn by the side of the road. There were several horse drawn carts parked outside and a battered, faded orange Volkswagen with a missing rear bumper and cardboard over the rear driver's side window. The doorway led into a large tavern area with a semicircular bar against the far wall. Men were seated at several tables drinking and smoking. The dimly lit room was permeated with thick, floating, grey smoke and Jake had to pause to stop from coughing.

Irkut had assured Jake that it was okay to bring in the 'slut', as he called her, and Jake held the leash attached to her collar as they walked in. She was still hooded and bound and her tattooed belly and chest advertised her to all what she was. A few eyes drifted to her superior form, but then went back to their discussions and their booze.

Irkut sidled up to the bar and Jake followed him. The Russian barked a monosyllabic command to the slave girl and she descended to her knees. Jake tied the leash off on the leg of his barstool and sat down. The barmaid was a fiftyish, heavy set woman with a fat, puffed face and graying brown hair pulled back behind her head in a bun. She had humorous, big brown eyes that seemed to be surprised at the visit from two strangers, one obviously a foreigner. She wiped the bar in front of the men and said in the local Kalikistani dialect, "What poisons for you, cousins?"

Irkut, the multilinguist, ordered two large flagons of the local ale and glasses of straight vodka on the side. When the broad hipped, merry woman had set them up and collected Irkut's coins, she spoke up. "Are you lost, cousins?"

"Only our souls are lost, Mother," Irkut replied. He grabbed the glass with its two inches of vodka and poured it back into his throat. Jake watched him, amazed, as usual. These people sure could drink, he thought. So as not to seem a wimp, he tossed his back too. Liquid fire poured down his throat and he coughed in spite of himself.

The barmaid laughed heartily. "Your little brother should stick to ale," she said to Irkut. Jake knew that her amusement was at his expense, but he remained silent.

"I'm teaching him how to be a man," Irkut replied, grinning back at the doughy fleshed woman. "We need beds for tonight," he told her. "Preferably ones that your horse hasn't slept in."

"We have fine rooms with soft mattresses," she replied, not bothered by Irkut's banter. "I'll have to get the pigs out of them though."

"Pigs I don't mind," Irkut replied.

The two laughed. "Twenty zlotskis each," she told Irkut. Zlotskis were the local currency, worthless outside the country.

"Done," Irkut replied. "And dinner?"

"There's a fine stew. Three zlotskis a bowl. But we don't feed *dévushki* in the bar." She was referring to the whore slave girl.

Irkut looked behind him at the naked, young hooded woman kneeling on the floor. "The whore belongs to my friend," he told her. "She'll eat upstairs."

"Three zlotskis for her too," The woman instructed Irkut. "I'll have her brought up after I feed you. But tell your foreign friend, no blood on the sheets."

Irkut grunted. After the woman went into the back room to get the stew, Irkut explained to Jake what was going on. Jake was surprised that the naked slave girl had prompted so little comment. But then he noticed in the dim light of the tavern a thin, almost emaciated, dark skinned woman sitting at the corner of the bar. She was naked too, and a chain ran from her nose to a ring set in the edge of the bar. She had dark, sad, hollow eyes and looked to be in her thirties. She bore the tell tale tattoo of a slave girl across her chest. Her hair was long and seemed greasy and unbrushed. A somewhat faded, spread winged, black falcon with grasping claws and an angry, wide open beak appeared on her belly. There was little life in her face. A thick leather collar ran around her throat.

The barmaid returned with the stew and plunked it down with two large stainless steel soupspoons. It had large chunks of meat and potatoes, carrots and peas swimming in a thick, brown sauce. Jake wondered what the meat was, but it did smell good. The barmaid went back into the kitchen and returned with another bowl. She dropped in front of the forlorn woman chained to the bar and issued a churlish order to her as she unlocked the chain from the ring. The woman picked it up and, with the loose chain dangling between her small, pointy breasts walked over to where Jake was sitting. She uttered a low, suppliant phrase that Jake did not understand. Irkut growled a response to her. Timidly, she took the end of the leash from Jake's stool and then tugged Jake's slave girl to her feet. She walked her across the room and urged her up a narrow flight of wooden steps, the bowl of stew balanced precariously in her other hand. The men in the room watched the slave girl's firm, naked, white bum as she hesitatingly ascended to the second floor. They then returned again to their drinks.

The stew was good and the ale was hearty. The men lingered over their meal without discussion. Jake could hear soft, low, male conversation from the scarred and ragged wooden tables behind him. He was wearing a light sport jacket over his polo shirt and he was glad to have his .38 tucked into his waistband behind his back. He mentally went over the procedure for ducking and pulling it out a few times. Irkut had brought in the suitcase in which they kept their euros and there was still half a million in there. It was more than enough for someone to die for and

Jake didn't want it to be him. Irkut didn't carry a pistol, but had a broad bladed, razor sharp knife in his boot.

The men were on their third ale and their third glass of fiery vodka when the brown haired slave girl returned. She carried the empty bowl back to the kitchen and returned to her perch at the end of the bar. The barmaid unceremoniously relocked her chain to the ring.

Jake was getting quite randy, thinking of the blond girl waiting for him up in his room. The tiny, quarter sized, weathered nipples of the brown haired slave's breasts reminded him of the thick, voluptuous ones waiting for him. He had fucked the girl the night before, after the party and the memory of her pliant, willing flesh almost made him swoon, an effect no doubt brought on by the hot vodka he had poured down his throat and the cool, almost bitter ale. Irkut was looking at the bar slave too.

"How much for the slut for the night?" he asked the fat barmaid finally.

"Thirty zlotskis," the woman replied as if she had just been waiting for the question.

"And for a blow job?" Irkut inquired.

"Thirty zlotskis," the woman repeated.

Irkut laughed. "And how much for you?"

"Sixty zlotskis," she replied smiling broadly. "But you'll have to pay my husband. He's at the table behind you."

Irkut looked over at three gnarled looking men sitting at the table nearest them and Jake followed his gaze, not knowing what was up, but figuring that Irkut had crossed some forbidden line. The one in the middle looked the meanest and he was the one who spoke. "In advance!"

Irkut and the barmaid broke out in hearty laughs. "Done!" Irkut shouted. There was laughter throughout the tavern. Jake felt left out but figured that he didn't want to know anyway. "I'm going upstairs," he told Irkut. "Let me have the bag."

Smiling, Irkut handed him the attaché case. As he walked to the stairs the barmaid called out to him in English, "Keep your money under the bed, *Americanski*." The room erupted in laughter again.

Jake guessed that the first room at the top of the stairs was his. When he entered he saw the buxom beauty standing in the middle of the room on her tip toes. The hood was still in place and there was a rope around her neck tied off to a rafter. He could hear her whining behind her gag. Jake realized that the lanky, almost emaciated, brunette slave had strung her up like this and had probably eaten the stew as well. Jake knew that he should relieve the girl's suffering, but the image of the helpless blond made his cock rise. He stepped up to her and took her large breasts in his hands. All firm and soft at the same time, they flowed through his fingers as he caressed them. The girl struggled on her toes, her thigh muscles tensed and stretched.

"I own this flesh," Jake thought and his passion began to rise. He released the girl's neck and she fell into his arms. He carried her over to the large, soft bed and laid her down. Her chest heaved as she tried to recover her starved breath. Jake place his lips on one of her broad, fat nipples and inhaled it into his mouth, suckling the teat, while his hand descended over the slave girl's hard, flat belly to the crux of her legs. He caressed the smooth hairless nether lips and slid his finger down the length of her slit. Trained as a whore, the girl obediently spread her thighs and raised her hips to meet Jake's probing hand. In a moment, her smooth, bare sex began to moisten and Jake gained entry to the girl's hot, tight crevasse. She moaned as he divided her engorging lower lips and spread her gathering moisture over her hardened pleasure bud.

His cock stiff and ready, Jake stood and tore his clothes from his body. When disrobed, he climbed back on the broad bed, its soft, white sheets melding with the pale white skin of the girl. The black hood which remained on her head stood in contrast to the sea of white under her. Jake placed his hand back on the girl's belly, sliding it across the angry, tattooed dragon that was etched there, poised to attack. He watched as her hands, confined to her sides by the stiff, brown leather belt, writhed in anticipation of her ravishment. He placed himself between her open thighs and presented his blood filled rod to her soft, wet, hairless opening. He could hear her sigh as he pressed the lips apart with the bulbous head of his cock. She raised her knees and thrust her pelvis at him and he lowered his manhood into her welcoming sheath.

The soft, warm flesh inside transmitted a wave of pleasure through Jake's body. Poised above the now moaning girl, his hand pressed into the mattress on either side of her shoulders, Jake could see her stiffened nipples, the blotch of redness that denoted her own arousal amidst the blue tattooed, Cyrillic letters across her chest. Slowly, gently, Jake ploughed the tight opening, reveling in the heat around his sword of flesh. He moaned as he plunged deeply within the girl's womb, burying his prick to its hilt.

"I own this flesh," Jake repeated to himself and his lust began to overcome him. He quickened his pace, his need upon him. As he thrust himself repeatedly within the girl's hot cavity, he dragged his cock across her stiff nub of pleasure causing the girl to squirm and moan. He wanted her to come. He wanted his property to perform for him. His cock was a tool to drive the slave girl nearer and nearer to sexual release. She thrust back at him, her heels planted firmly into the bed, her breasts swaying and shifting, recording her body's tremors. Her breath was coming harder and harder, her moans growing louder.

Suddenly her body jerked and her moan became a cry, muffled by the leather gag under her black hood. Her body began to shiver and her cunt clamped Jake's cock tightly. "Mmmmmmmmpf! Mmmmmmmmpf! Mmmmmmmmpf!" she cried out as her orgasm shot through her body. Jake watched her intently. His hooded slave girl, her face and all that it could express obscured, could be any woman, was all women. His climax suddenly upon him, Jake pressed his chest against the pillowy flesh of the slave girl's breasts and grabbed her shoulders tightly. "Aaaaaaagh! Aaaaaaagh!" he roared as he pounded his hips into the girl's. "Aaaaaagh! Aaaaaaagh!" he shouted, his voice reverberating throughout the room. His fluids jetted into the girl's throbbing crevasse, each pulse of pleasure causing Jake's body to convulse.

When he had finally emptied himself inside the girl, Jake felt a wave of relief flood him. His body sagged against the girl's, limp and satiated.

It took Jake a couple of minutes to recover. Slowly, he rolled off of his property and lay flat on his back. He had never felt so satisfied. His mind began to darken into sleep as a result of the expenditure of his lust and the effects of the alcohol he had drunk. The girl lay next to him, panting.

An hour later, Jake awoke with a start. For a moment he panicked and tried to remember where he had left his weapon. The room was still lit by the small table lamp by the door. When he recovered his senses, Jake realized that the girl next to him was squirming and rocking her hips. His own filled bladder brought home to him the cause of the girl's distress. He rose quickly from the bed and pulled the slave girl to her feet. The room had no bathroom, but there was a large chamber pot on the dresser. Jake placed the pot on the floor and removed its lid. He maneuvered the girl so that her legs were straddling it and pushed on her shoulders. The girl obediently squatted and, after he gently stroked her hairless sex, emitted a hard, yellow stream. He could hear her sigh as the fluids left her. What had not occurred to him occurred to him now. He had the freedom to dispose of this beautiful, young woman's flesh as he saw fit, but he also had the obligation to see to her needs. She was a source of pleasure and a responsibility. Without his command and care she would suffer needlessly, with pleasure or profit to no one.

Jake then realized that the girl had neither eaten nor drunk since they left the estate. Wiping her sex with a cloth napkin from the dresser, Jake pushed her to a seated position on the bed. He untied the string which held the black hood over the girl's head and removed it. Two grateful but wary eyes emerged. He then loosened the gag and removed the thick leather plug from her mouth. He stepped to the dresser and filled a cup from a pitcher of water that was standing there. He brought it over to the girl to drink.

The girl took the water greedily as Jake presented the cup to her lips. When she had finished the second glass, Jake remembered his own need for relief and emptied his bladder into the chamber pot, mixing his fluids with hers.

Jake decided to try and get his charge something to eat. Raising his finger in a signal to wait, he retrieved his pants and shirt and went down to the kitchen. The brunette slave girl was asleep in a cage in the corner of the room. Jake found some bread and brought that and two bottles of beer back to his room. He left a 10 zlotski note on the counter in payment

The slave girl was still sitting expectantly on the bed. Jake loosened her wrists from the belt around her waist and removed it. He handed her the large chunk of dark, rich bread. The girl seized it and began to devour it hungrily. As she took each bite, she would look up at her lord and master as if seeking permission for another mouthful.

When she had downed it, Jake offered her another cup of water which she consumed quickly.

Well, he had seen to the girl's basic needs. Now what? Jake was drinking one of the bottles of beer, enjoying its crisp, cool taste and admiring the fine, curvaceous flesh of his slave. He realized that he didn't know her name and asked her. It was the first question he had put to her, all his other words having been curt commands. He had not yet acquired the art of deciphering the strange Cyrillic writing on her chest. The steward, the day before, had said her name, but he had also said three others and Jake could not remember which one was the blonde's. The girl looked at him sheepishly, as if giving away her name would be just one bit more of power that this strange man had over her. In a way it was, since it required her to reveal some of her inner self. She hesitated and then uttered in a low, hesitant voice, "Klara, master."

Jake considered the name. German? Dutch? He asked her. "Dutch, master," she answered meekly. It was strange to find that the docile and obedient creature had a voice. Jake knew that there was a whole history behind the two words that the beautiful girl had spoken. She had once a home, friends, a family. He didn't want to know any of that.

"Stand up," he told her, signaling his desire with an upward wave of his hand. Dutifully, the girl arose from the big, soft bed and stood in front of him. Jake was short, about 5"6", and the girl reached just below the crown of his head in height. Her eyes were downcast and her face neutral. All rebellion had been removed from this creature many weeks ago and she was aware that initiative was not a positive quality for a slave. It was far better to wait for orders.

"Put your hands over your head," Jake commanded the girl. She looked up at him with confusion in her eyes.

"No good Englishe, master" she said timidly as if to ward off a punishment for being so dumb.

"So much for deep, soulful conversations," Jake thought to himself. He indicated to the fearful girl what he wanted by placing his own hands on his head and nodding to her. She complied quickly, a small smile of achievement on her face. The movement raised her large, melon sized breasts and Jake inspected them with appreciation. He placed his hands under them, assessing their fullness and ran his thumbs across the short, fat nipples. They stiffened at his command. The girl had broad, pale areola that seemed to fade away at the edges into the pale skin of her breasts.

Jake removed his hands and stepped around behind the girl. She had well defined back muscles and soft, round shoulders. Her back tapered down to a slim waist. Jake ran his hands along her back, enjoying the feel of her soft skin and tense muscles. Her ass was round and firm. The girl was standing with her legs wide apart, undoubtedly part of her training, and Jake slipped his hand between the girl's thighs from behind, seizing her soft mound. It was sticky from their commingled discharges. Jake softly stroked the tender lips that enclosed the girl's pleasure giving hole until he felt the girl stirring and the lips softened and began to dilate.

There was a mirror on the wall above the dresser and Jake pulled the girl over to it. He watched her pleasant, young face as his hand forced passion upon the girl. He grabbed one of her breasts from behind and pinched and played with the hardened nipple. He could see both the girl and himself in the mirror. Her face was softened, her eyes closed, her lips parted. Her tongue emerged from her mouth to wet her thick lips, leaving behind a glossy sheen. Jake wanted the girl to see him and ordered, "Open your eyes."

Klara's eyes opened in response. Jake didn't know whether she had understood the order or just reacted to the sound of command in his voice. He captured her eyes with his in the mirror. She seemed to understand his desire and kept her eyes open and glued to his. As his hand probed deeper and deeper into her loins, Klara's body began to rock slowly and her eyes began to mist. Jake felt the skin on her breast tighten as it filled with her aroused blood. He rubbed Klara's engorged clit with his fingers gently, circling around it, covering it with her pungent discharge.

In the mirror, Jake could see the girl struggling to keep her eyes open. Her lips tightened and her face grimaced as she tried to delay the inevitable. She was giving out little grunts now as her passions rose higher and higher. Jake could feel her thighs quiver with his hand and he began to stroke Klara's pleasure bud slowly and deliberately while her pulled hard on her nipple. Klara gripped her lips tightly together. Jake released her breast and squeezed her cheeks until her mouth opened again. She was trembling and she could not suppress the sounds of her arousal. "Oooooooo! Ooooooooooo!" she called out. "Ahhhhhhh! Ahhhhhhhhhh!" she cried. Her knees bent and a wave of release crossed her face. Her eyes begged Jake's to stop, or continue, or both. When she came, her thighs clamped tightly on Jake's wrist, her knees bent. Her breasts shook and swayed as the pulses of her orgasm ran through her. "Ooooooooooh! Ooooooooooooh!" she cried out again.

Jake's rod was hard again and he had seen enough. He pushed Klara towards the bed and shoved her torso forward until she had laid her forehead on it, her arms still bent, her hands planted firmly on her head. Jake, who was still dressed from his foray downstairs, released his cock from his pants and drove it deeply into the slave girl's wide open, well lubricated gash. Her legs were spread wide and Jake thrust up into her womb forcefully, urgently. His hands held tightly to her hips, holding her in place for his pleasures. Jake grunted loudly as he came, his cock throbbing, each spasm sending a jolt of electricity through him. The girl came too, her moans muffled by the mattress of which her face lay.

Jake stood, his softening cock impaling the still trembling woman. He inspected the tiny star between her rear cheeks and pledged himself to delve into its wonders soon enough. He ran his hands over her rear globes appreciatively, reveling in the soft skin.

Jake finally removed himself from his slave's slick cunt and began to prepare himself for the night. The money bag went under the bed as the barmaid had suggested and he collected his snub nosed .38 and placed it under his pillow. It was not good for target practice, but it made a loud noise and quite a mess at short range. Opening his suitcase, Jake removed one of his little toys. It was a miniature electronic door alarm, one of Irving's inventions, the two halves of which mounted on the edge of the door and the door jam respectively. It had a sticky bottom and so no screws or nails were necessary to install it. If the two halves were separated during the night by the opening of the door by more than a fraction of an inch, the alarm would sound loudly and Jake would immediately emerge from the bed, naked, but armed with his .38.

After setting the alarm, Jake removed his pants and shirt and climbed into the bed on the other side. He snapped his fingers and the girl rose from her prone position in which he left her and, at his hand signal slid beneath the sheets. Jake rolled her onto her stomach and attached her leather bracelets behind her back. No sense taking chances with a slave girl. She seemed docile and trained enough, but still waters ran deep and she might just take it into her head to sneak his pistol out from under his pillow and blow her rapist away.

* * * * * * * * * * * * * *

The night passed uneventfully and Jake awoke on his stomach, his arms buried under his pillow. One hand rested on the handle of his .38. He was surprised to find the body of the slave girl pressed up against him, her breasts mashed against his side, her long, graceful leg intertwined with his. He managed to extricate himself without waking her. Gentle dawn light was filtering through the window and it made the girl's pretty face seem almost angelic. She seemed at peace as she slept.

There was no shower in the room, the amenities of this countryside inn seeming to have stopped at electricity. He decided to dress and go downstairs to see what he could do by way of food and coffee. He took the valise with the money with him. When he reached the bar area he saw Irkut sitting at a stool drinking a large cup of steaming black coffee. The bar maid was sitting next to him, her fat arm over his small shoulder. She was dressed in a tent like white, cotton night gown with delicate, little, blue flowers. Her hair was down. She stirred when she heard Jake.

"Breakfast, *Americanski?*" she asked him, a huge smile across her face. Jake nodded and she got up from her stool. She went into the kitchen and returned with another large cup of strong, aromatic, black coffee and a bowl of steaming mush. It was some kind of oatmeal strewn with raisins and covered by a layer of a thick, sweet syrup. It came with a large, wooden spoon. "Eat, *Americanski,*" she said merrily. "You're almost as skinny as your hot blooded friend here." She patted Irkut on the head tenderly. Irkut looked up at her and smiled. He turned and looked at Jake almost sheepishly and shrugged his shoulders as if to excuse his weakness for large women.

The barmaid offered to have a bowl of mush sent up to the slave girl, but Jake demurred, remembering that last night the brunette slave had eaten it instead of feeding it to Klara. "I'll bring it up myself," he told her as he shoveled down a spoonful of the thick, gooey meal. He finished quickly and took a bowl and spoon up to his body slave. When he entered the room, she was kneeling on the floor across from the door, expectantly. She had a fearful expression on her face which Jake took as being guilt for having slept while her master had already awoken. Jake ignored it and put the bowl down on the floor next to her. He released her arms from behind her and told her, "Eat."

CHAPTER FIVE
THE DECK GETS RESHUFFLED

The crowd roared as Maddy and her cartmate notched another victory. This was a home crowd and the enthusiasm was just that much greater as even the least informed pony race fan knew that the points garnered from the victory brought Grobgy's estate just that much closer to a overall championship title. Vadim was pleased as he drove Lightning and Persephone around the track for a victory lap.

Things had reverted to almost normal after the brief interlude with the dwarf. Maddy had not seem him again and, except for the fact that she had to do some practice runs with the tall, lanky ponygirl in Persephone's place, all was as it should be. Vadim rubbed both of his ponies down after each day of practice and used his experienced and knowledgeable tongue to drive them both to ecstasy as they lay face up on the training table, their legs spread wide, their hips cocked at just the right angle, to receive his oral caresses. Maddy squirmed and moaned as the rough, hot tongue of her driver plunged her depths and worried the little nubbin of flesh at the apex of her sex. She found it hard to remember when her life was not driven by the need for sex.

She had been transformed in more ways than one and her empty canal often yearned for the presence of a stiff, male member. The fingers and tongues of her driver, his slave girl and her fellow pony, Persephone, left her well pleasured but yearning. She had not had a cock in her driving her to pleasure since the opening day of race season when her owner had taken his rights with her. She did not count her punishment of a few days before since, while she was being ploughed by the many unknown men, she had been in misery, the thought that she had failed her driver inhibiting her satisfaction. Her owner had used her rear entrance once on her first race day, and while she had relished in his presence within her, she had been disappointed when he had left her dripping cunt empty.

It was a small price to pay, though, for the tranquility and comfort of her driver's care. There was still a part of her that rebelled at the anonymous and callous use of her openings, part of her that tried to remember that she was a 21st century woman with the right to determine her own destiny, to control her own body.

The driver's slave girl was just releasing Maddy and Persephone from harness when she heard a great moan emanate from the racing paddock which lay out of sight over a little rise from the pony camp ground. Maddy had guessed from the timing of the return of the sulky cart after each race with its prancing, victorious pony, a garland around its neck, that the sulky race, she did not call it that, she did not know what to call it, followed hers. Something had happened during the one pony race, she thought. When she looked at the pale, unhappy face of her driver, she was sure.

Drabik had watched as Starlight came around the 1200 meter turn. She was leading her opponent by half a cart and the dwarf was driving her madly. All of a sudden, just as she entered the home stretch, just as she was beginning to put some real distance between her and the other pony, she seemed to leap into the air. Her head, blue and gold hooded for racing day, jerked backwards and she collapsed to her knees, fell forward and ploughed the track with her face. The sulky cart almost tipped over on top of her and Jerzi, her driver, had to hold onto the sides of it to prevent being sent head over heels. He jumped down off of the cart and began to belabor the prone pony mercilessly with his whip. It was useless, as the other pony was already almost at the finish line.

Grobgy was also in the stands, in the owner's box. He attended almost all of the pony races, taking the time off from his nefarious pursuits whenever he could. He threw the racing program that he had carefully marked up with his observations and suggestions for his racing crews onto the floor. "Shit!" he yelled. He had gambled and he had lost. He looked through his binoculars and could see the pony writhing in agony on the ground. She had undoubtedly reinjured her knee ligaments. She was certainly down for the season, maybe forever. He fingered the handle of the Makerov that he kept holstered to his waist at all times, resisting the urge to descend from the stands and put down the pony that had disappointed him so greatly. It was done from time to time, an enraged owner striding purposely out to the track fiddling at his waist. But it was not good for the crowd, especially with regard to a favorite like Starlight, and at home, too. If this had been an away match he might just have done it.

But sense prevailed and he got up and climbed carefully down the grandstand steps to the track. He purposely kept his hand from his waist and signaled the emergency crew to roll out the ambulance cart. The crowd cheered as they saw the flatbed cart drawn by two hefty, blue hooded ponies run out onto the track. The cheered again when Starlight was lifted up on to it and carted back to the pony camp.

Drabik took secret pleasure in the injury to the sulky pony. He knew that Lightning would now be moved up to the sulky class and be handed over to the dark methods of Jerzi and his notoriously cruel brother. Lightning had brought out something in him that he thought was dead. For weeks now, he had longed to place his hands on her sleek flanks, to bury himself inside her. He had trained dozens of ponies and had never given a flying fuck for any

of them. They were no longer women; they were beasts
and deserved to live only as long as they were useful. But
with Lightning, it was something different. He dreamed of
her, yearned for her plump lips on his cock, yearned to
watch her writhe with pleasure at his behest, his manhood
sunk deep in her rear. The fact that she had found a
relative, temporal paradise in the hands of Vadim drove
him wild. She should be suffering for what she had done
to him. He smiled, knowing that now she would suffer.
And when she returned to his care in a few weeks, she
would be just another broken, terrorized female, devoid of
personality. Maybe then he could stop thinking of her as
part human.

Later that day, they came for Maddy. She had just
been showered by the little blond slave girl. Maddy had
spent the afternoon with a dreadful sense of foreboding.
When she saw Drabik and the dwarf enter Vadim's camp,
the tall pony from the other day in tow, her throat
constricted with fear. Without fanfare, she was unhooked
from the back of Vadim's trailer and attached to a leash in
the gnarled hand of the fearsome, little man. Without a
goodbye from Vadim or a chance to nuzzle her erstwhile
lover, Persephone, she was led away.

Jerzi's trailer and encampment was on the other side of
the pony park. Maddy trudged behind her captor in a state
of abject despair. How many times would her life worsen,
she asked herself. When would this surreal nightmare end?

When they reached Jerzi's trailer, Drabik, who had
accompanied them, turned to the naked, bound pony girl
and took her nipples in his hands. He smiled and said
something to her in Russian, pinching the nipples hard.
Maddy winced behind her hood and a deep chasm opened
in her belly. Her trainer released her and, waiving to the
scar faced dwarf, walked away.

Jerzi had tied Maddy's leash off to the side of his van. A small, black haired, naked slave girl, wearing the ubiquitous shield gag over her lower face, her hair cut short, red stripes and black and blue marks distributed over her pale skin, was kneeling next to the van, her head bowed, her arms poised behind her. The dwarf uttered a sharp command to her and she sprang to her feet. She ran and got a ladder and placed it against the side of the van. She climbed it and swung out a heavy metal arm and locked it in place so that it stood out perpendicular from the vehicle. Maddy felt the Dwarf behind her unfastening her wrists.

Maddy could think of only one reason why her wrists would be unbound. During her training, they were often unlocked and refastened to a training table so that her aching back muscles could be rubbed and massaged. But that was clearly not the purpose now. The other times that her wrists had been freed were so that they could be fastened over her head to a chain prefatory to a fierce beating. As her wrists were rejoined before her and then pulled up over her head by a chain connected to the steel arm that extended from the van, Maddy's worst fears were confirmed. She began to cry in fear and she actually lost control of her bladder, her urine streaming down her legs. When she saw the small, evil looking man emerge from the van with a long, leather switch, she began to whine.

The first blow landed across Maddy's defenseless breasts. It was like a hot poker had been dragged across them. The helpless ponygirl screamed in pain. The next blow created a line of fire across her belly and she began to dance from foot to foot, crying and begging for mercy. The dwarf had a fierce, determined aspect and his eyes gleamed each time he reared back his small arm and unleashed the fury of the whip against Maddy's skin. There was enough room between Maddy and the trailer that the dwarf could strike any part of Maddy's body at will, and he alternated between her back and front. She felt the excruciating bite of the lash across the back and front of her thighs, across her shins and on her pale, white rear globes. Her breasts burned as if afire as the lash repeatedly found its target there. Her back was crisscrossed with trails of bright red wounds. "Ahhhhhhhhhh! Ahhhhhhhhhhh!" Maddy cried, her voice muffled by her leather gag, as again and again the dwarf belabored her innocent flesh.

The ponygirl had done nothing wrong. She had not failed in her duties. She was being taught a vital lesson by the small but powerful man. He was in command of her now. Her idyll was over. She would dedicate, from here on in, her whole being to the cruel man's will.

Jerzi left Maddy hanging by her arms for several hours. Her arms had not been pulled taut above her since her muscles would have strained had her full weight been placed upon them. While once Maddy's arms were firm and trim, the hardness had turned to flab through disuse. She despaired at how weak and useless they felt. She doubted that she could even lift them of her own accord.

Finally, the dwarfish man allowed his timid, obsequious, slave girl to release Maddy's arms. The ponygirl fell to her knees, grateful that the aching in her diminished upper limbs could cease. The dwarf locked them again behind her and then pushed her forwards so that her blue hooded face was in the dirt. Maddy heard him issue his slave girl a rude order and she heard the unzipping of his pants behind her. She could hear the telltale slurping of a mouth sucking a cock. The dwarf was getting himself hard for her. After a few moments, she felt him kneel down behind her and present his hardened cock to her supple, yet narrow rear opening. Maddy was prepared to serve her new overlord, but was surprised, given his diminutive stature, at how thick his manhood was. She whined as she felt her rear opening stretched. In spite of the pain, she was waiting for the delightful feel of a man's hardness scraping across her tight anal ring, anticipated the creaming of her sex, the hard, intense orgasm that normally followed. But this time, it was not to be. Jerzi was performing another ritual. He was demonstrating his compete mastery of her. She would serve his pleasure, not he hers. As a result of the black haired slave girl's skilled manipulation of the small man's cock, he was ready to explode once he had plugged his long, thick manhood deep inside Maddy's bowels. She felt his hot seed spurt inside her, the throbbing of his piece, the hard grip of his rough hands on her hips. He grunted as he came. He then withdrew while still hard. Maddy, abject and forlorn, deprived of any opportunity for sexual pleasure, could hear the slave girl cleaning the callous dwarf's tool off with her lips.

Afterwards, after kneeling in the sun for some time, her back arched, her forehead planted in the grass, Maddy felt the small, soft hands of the slave girl urge her to her feet. The girl showered her and fed her. Maddy tried to look into the eyes of the black haired girl, but the busy slave girl avoided her gaze. Maddy was able to see the deadness in the girl's eyes, undoubtedly put there by the cruel abuses of her master. She realized that her life with the dwarf was to be totally unlike her life with her prior driver. There would be no tender caresses from the black haired girl. There would be no Persephone to cuddle with. And how and when her driver used her would have nothing to do with his concern for her pleasure.

Just as the slave girl had finished drying her off, Maddy saw the dwarf come back into view through the tiny holes in her hood. She sensed the slave girl's fearful stiffening of her body. She found that her own body followed suit. The dwarf stood before the cowering females and then snapped his fingers. Maddy and the slave girl both fell to their knees obediently. He gave an order to the slave girl who rose and removed Maddy's gag. Maddy watched as the small, but fearsome man withdrew his fat, long, limpid cock from his pants. He presented it to his new pony. Maddy obediently shuffled closer to the man on her knees and, bending low, took the flaccid meat into her mouth.

She had started to work the man's tool with her tongue and lips when she felt a yank at the back of her head. He had taken hold of her pony tail and was twisting it painfully. Maddy was confused. Didn't he want his cock sucked? Was she doing it wrong? As his grip eased, Maddy began to massage the soft, hot meat in her mouth again only to feel her hair yanked back again. The dwarf pulled his cock from her mouth and slapped her hooded face hard twice. Maddy was terrorized that he would beat her again and parsed her mind desperately to discern the man's desire. The familiar empty feeling was back in her stomach and she tried to blink back her fear induced tears. Again he presented his cock to Maddy's mouth. She opened it receptively and brought the soft flesh within. This time, however, she allowed the limp manhood to rest on her tongue. She dared not presume to do more without a clear affirmative signal from her master.

This was, in fact, the precise effect that Jerzi intended. He held the pony's head still and let the warmth of the passive mouth excite him. Maddy could feel the man's appendage beginning to grow hard in her mouth. She would never have expected such a large tool on such a small man and was disconcerted at the apparent anomaly. The prick began to expand with blood and lengthen as it lay between her passive lips. It was growing as if by magic, as if by the sheer will of its owner alone. He kept her face buried against his belly and the prick began to push at the back of Maddy's throat at the same time that it distended her mouth.

When the man's cock had become thick and long, Maddy felt his grip on her ponytail tighten again. She felt her head pulled back until the fat, round head of the cock lay upon her tongue. Her lips still gripped its shaft tightly. She felt the man begin to stroke that part of his prick that lay outside her mouth. His hand worked quickly, from time to time knocking against her lips and mouth. Still Maddy did nothing to assist the man's pleasure but remain still, her tongue depressed flat in her mouth. Finally, she heard the dwarf grunt with pleasure. His hand began to ride frantically on his meat. Maddy tasted the semi-sweet release of his precum. He was going to discharge in her mouth, not as a response to Maddy's now quite skilled oral efforts, but on his own, her mouth merely a receptacle for his spunk. "Argh!" the little man grunted once and Maddy felt and tasted the viscous discharge of his cock on her tongue.

The next morning, Maddy was put through an intense workout by her new driver. She ran and ran and ran until she thought that she would drop. Her back and rear burned from his whip. The second day was the same. She winced each time that she was driven out of the pony camp and passed her former encampment. She had a glimpse of Persephone being harnessed to the yearling cart together with the long, tall pony who had replaced her. Her mind clouded over with misery as she dutifully pulled her new apparatus past. When not training, Maddy spent most of time locked in a tiny cage, a large, black cloth draped over it. And the dwarf continued to use her callously, without regard to her pleasure.

On the third day, she was packed into the rear of the dwarf's pony van and carted on a four hour trip to the next race. She cantered behind her former cartmate in the pre-race pony parade. She was beaten easily by the sulky pony she raced against and received a thorough and exquisite beating from her driver as a result. There were two more days of relentless and painful practice and then another race, which she lost as well. It was not as if Maddy was not trying. Filled with misery and terror, she dug her boots deep into the track and pumped her legs with as much energy and determination she could find. But her driver was not pleased and her life continued to be a gauntlet of pain and abuse.

Oddly enough, Maddy's appearance in the spring championship tournament was assured. Starlight had amassed enough victories to be included and Maddy was seconded to her record based on Starlight's inability to compete due to injury. But Jerzi knew his ponies well. He had been pleasantly surprised when had had first ridden Maddy and knew what she could do. She didn't yet, but, he resolved, she would.

It was in the third race, ten days after Maddy had fallen from heaven into hell that it happened. She knew when she trotted down to the track for her race that this day would be different. She had developed a steel hard core, her body and mind were intensely focused on her need to win. Her opponent was a long legged, Italian pony who had a long string of victories and who Maddy would undoubtedly see again in the Spring Tournament, although she could not know it, being totally ignorant of the tournament or any part of her future. Perhaps her driver was overconfident, expecting an easy race against the upstart yearling. Grobgy was in the stands that day as was Drabik, who was acting as his bodyguard. From the owner's box they watched as the two sulkies were negotiated into their starting positions. Drabik looked out at his former charge through his binoculars. He could see her nervous pawing at the ground, the slight shivering of her tautly held head. The meet so far was close and Grobgy needed to win either the 1500 meter or the 3000 meter sulky to carry the day. The 3000 meter would be tight. The other estate had the edge. Jerzi had assured Grobgy that Lightning would soon break out. Grobgy gripped his own binoculars tightly. "Maybe today is the day," he thought hopefully.

When the starting gun went off, Maddy got a jump on the other pony. You could have gone home right there. She led the other sulky by a length at the quarter pole and by a length and a half at the midmark. By the time they came down the home stretch Maddy was two cart lengths ahead.

The exhausted ponygirl's heart almost burst with joy as she crossed the finish line. The crowd in the grandstands was madly wild with the upset, cheering and chanting her name, "*Molnya! Molnya! Molnya!*" as she finished her victory lap and entered the winner's circle. Grobgy came down and nuzzled her breasts, smiling, his thick black moustache spreading across his face. Even Drabik was thrilled. He knew that she could do it. He had known it from the beginning. He watched the pony's still heaving chest with pride.

Maddy pranced back to the pony camp, the victory garlands around her neck, to wild applause. But her heart darkened as she reached the dwarf's campground. It was a place of fear and torment and even her victory could not make her forget it. The black haired slave girl unhooked her from the cart and removed her harness and garland. The small driver stood and watched. He gave a command and Maddy sank to her knees obediently. Her knowledge of Russian was limited to these one word commands, but she knew them well as she knew well the punishments for not complying with these directives immediately. The dwarf gave the black haired girl an instruction and Maddy felt leather straps connecting her high, stiff, black leather boots to her thighs. She then pushed Maddy's torso back until her shoulders touched the ground behind her. Her thighs and feet were imprisoned beneath her. Her fleshy but firm breasts were pointed at the sky. She felt her nipples harden with fear. What new torment was she to face now, she thought. She had won, hadn't she? Wasn't that the point? Why was she to be beaten now? Fear crept through her and her eyes began to tear. "Why? Why? Why?" she asked God piteously.

Suddenly, she felt the naked thighs of her cruel driver press in between hers. She felt the head of his thick, stiff prick ply along the length of her hairless slit. His thumb began to nudge the hood to her pleasure bud and Maddy's juices began to flow. He was going to fuck her! Maddy spread her thighs wide in eager anticipation. She wanted his steel like rod to pierce her, wanted the reward that she had strived so hard to deserve. When she felt his cock begin to press aside the tingling outer lips of her sex, the ponygirl moaned with appreciation. Her lusts had been pent up for the better part of a week, lusts that had been made such an integral part of her that she could not remember a time when she had not yearned madly for completion.

The racing bit was still lodged tightly in Maddy's mouth and her moan escaped as the dwarf drove himself deeper and deeper inside her. Her body was covered with a sheen of sweat and her thighs quivered and shook with expectation. When her driver began a slow, deliberate stroke within her, Maddy began to pant and whine with need.

For the first time since she had been in his thrall, the dwarf was serving Maddy's body. He drew his tool across Maddy's clit slowly, forcefully, feeling the half beast, half woman writhe and shiver beneath him. His short frame was just long enough that he could reach Maddy's breasts with his lips and he inhaled her right nipple and suckled at it intently. The hot lips of her driver on her teat drove Maddy over the top and she moaned and grunted in ecstatic pleasure as her body convulsed with each hard, intense contraction of her pussy. Her orgasm subsided, but the Dwarf kept going, raising her lusts once more, driving the pony mad with desire. She thrust her hips back at the tiny man's as best she was able with her legs locked beneath her, and her mouth approximated exclamations of lust as she was driven over the precipice once again. He did not relent until his pony had come for a third, mind reeling time. Maddy was writhing and twisting beneath him as he allowed his own lust to build and sprayed jet after jet of his hot cum deeply into her womb. Maddy received it with joy for the first time since she had been condemned to his care. She had swallowed his slimy white discharge, he had emptied himself into her pussy and rear, but this was the first time that she had felt the soothing, warm flow of his liquid inside her while in the throes of passion.

* * * * * * * * * * * * * * * * *

In the dingy, cement block lined walls of a warehouse basement in Elizabeth, New Jersey, blond haired, long legged Mary Ellen Perskiowski was sitting on top of a small desk, her well toned, gracefully formed, bare legs spread wide. She had been given the job of supervising the stateside slave operation while Jake was in Kalikastan. She had recruited six other dangerous, unscrupulous and, as it happened, beautiful, young women to assist her and for the past three months they had been collecting kidnapped young women across the Eastern part of the United States as far away as Michigan and Missouri. A new batch had been unloaded tonight and they were confined in tiny cages that lined one of the walls in the long, narrow basement. They were hooded and gagged and had small plugs stuck in their ears to minimize their awareness of what was going on around them. This way a slip of the tongue of their jailers would not result in the release of any forbidden information such as names or their location.

Working assiduously between Mary Ellen's knees was the abject young woman whose fate it was to remain constantly imprisoned in the basement and to service the pretty young, slave girls to be. She remained in a nude state all of the time and had a collar around her neck that connected via a chain to a pipe that hung from the ceiling and ran the length of the cellar. This way she could remain chained and confined but still have the ability to travel the length of the tiny cages to water, feed or clean the wastes from the frightened, helpless girls. She was thin and had stringy, long, black hair. She wore a leather collar and leather bracelets around her wrists and ankles.

Her name was Allison, and she was the former girlfriend of one of the slavers whose interests in the slave operation had been recently fatally terminated. In what she knew now had been a colossal mistake, Allison had tried to break up with the slaver, a mean, unscrupulous Irishman named Feeney, and he had one night, on a pretext, led her down to this dungeon. Four of his men had been waiting there, expectantly. She had been here ever since, for about two years.

Allison was used as a communal whore by the lords of this domain. The new girls were largely to go untouched. Their new owners would want them as pristine as the day they were snatched. But Allison was available to succor the unavoidable lusts that arose from the presence of so many naked, defenseless, beautiful, young women. Feeney and the male members of his gang had used her at their pleasure and Mary Ellen and her girls had followed their example. Allison didn't mind. The women were not as cruel and she preferred licking their hot, moist cunts to being rudely plugged by the men's stiff, hard, cocks.

Mary Ellen sighed as the girl's experienced tongue ran the length of her slit. Mary Ellen had long, straw blond hair and her bush, although well trimmed, was still a wiry, thick thatch. She absentmindedly ran her hand through her pubic hair as Allison excited her slit. Mary Ellen, who was more inclined to wearing tight fitting slacks, now always donned one of her more revealing miniskirts when she knew she was coming down to the cellar. It was easier to just shed her thong than to pull tight pants over her feet. She sighed deeply as the dark haired slave girl deftly tickled her hardened clit with her tongue.

Her passion upon her, Mary Ellen took both hands and pressed them on Allison's obedient head. She liked to have her tongue squirming deeply inside her when she orgasmed and had instructed Allison on the proper technique. She moaned deeply, her long, sleek legs shuddering as she came.

She patted Allison's head when she was finished, her pulsing cunt calmed. "Okay, slut, back in your cage for now," she told the black haired girl. Allison dutifully rose to her feet and scurried the one hundred foot length of the room to find her cage. She crawled into it and pulled the door shut behind her, locking it. She would not be released until one of the other gangster women required her services or it was necessary to tend to the other imprisoned females.

About a half hour earlier, Mary Ellen had been on a scrambled telephone conversation with her employer, Mr. Burnham. Mary Ellen was a little disconcerted that Burnham had cut Jake out of the loop. Jake had hired Mary Ellen and her team of cutthroat lesbians. She trusted Jake. He was a cold motherfucker, but he was loyal and always got the job done. She didn't know Burnham from a hole in the ground. But it was clear that he was in man in charge and she had to be at least polite to him.

Burnham had told her that he was interested in expanding operations. He wanted to extend their reach to the western states and even California and Canada. He had explained that the new pipeline construction in Kalikastan was going to create a huge demand for compliant slave girls and that they needed to increase the supply to maintain market share. Mary Ellen was having none of it. This operation was the limits of what she would do. A woman had to have some standards after all. The girls that she helped process, loading them in specially designed air cargo containers for air shipment to Kalikastan, had already been captured by someone else. If Jake and his crew had not taken over the Elizabeth, New Jersey operation, these unfortunate young women would have been here bound and gagged and destined for unhappy, short lives anyway. But to expand operations, to increase the flow of unhappy females went against her grain. No, she had told him. She would not assist in recruiting other teams. She and Jake had agreed that what she was doing was only for the sake of the mission, the recovery of Burnham's niece. After that, they would shut it down.

* * * * * * * * * * * * *

Jake was not a happy camper. He had returned to Burnham's estate after completing a few more purchases with his beautiful, young, slave girl in tow. They had still not spoken more than one or two word sentences to each other, Klara being understandably reticent to demonstrate loquaciousness. Jake was not inclined to delve too far into the psyche of his enslaved lover either. But he reveled in her flesh. During the ten days of the balance of his trip he had used her body in as many ways as he could think of. He had taken to petting her tenderly when they lay abed following a tempestuous bout of sex. She was a passionate wench indeed, and never quailed at his demands. She sucked him lovingly it seemed at times, taking twenty or thirty minutes to slowly drive her master and lord to orgasm. Only once had he seen what might have been interpreted as a smile from her. Jake had spent an hour between her thighs, caressing her plush sex with his tongue and lips. After each of her many orgasms, he would rest a while, letting her recover from her passionate, loud response and then begin again. She alternated digging her heels firmly in the mattress, her legs splayed widely as she thrust her hips up at him, and clamping his head firmly with her sleek, tender thighs as she moaned and writhed under his ministrations. Afterwards, her normally neutral, emotionless face softened when she looked at him.

But now they were back at the estate and he would have to do something with her. Burnham had been effusive in his praise of her pulchritude and had entreated him to let him try her out. Jake had hesitated. She was his and he wanted her to stay that way. But, on the other hand, she was a slave girl. He couldn't take her back to the States. And he reviled himself for coming to care too much about her. Besides, he had already let Irkut have his way with her more than once, watching while he ploughed her from the rear at some roadside campground where they had stopped to have their lunch.

But that was not what was really bothering him. It was the cold, hard faces of Burnham's new security team that was disconcerting. He spoke to Burnham about it in private.

"Mr. Burnham," he told his employer, "you seem to be surrounding yourself with some pretty unsavory characters. Do you know what you're doing?"

"Oh, come off it Jake," Burnham replied impatiently. "I've got a huge investment in this country now. And I'll be damned if I'm going to let one of these bush league gangsters put the arm on me. Without a security team I'd be open season for any of the local bandits."

"But the Commission...." Jake started to say.

"The Commission, nothing," Burnham replied. "They may control the capital and the distribution of graft, but this is still a village based culture. Those guys are essentially tribal leaders and their writ doesn't extend very far. Once the money stops flowing from the pipeline, they may have a wholly different attitude towards me anyway."

"But we'll be gone long before that," Jake protested. "I'm sure I'll find Maddy soon. It's just a matter of time."

"Jake," Burnham said, his voice authoritative and firm. "You don't get it. I'm not going anywhere. I'm moving my headquarters here and I intend to live like a Turkish Emir until my cock goes limp permanently."

Jake looked at the naked, brown haired slave girl kneeling next to Burnham's desk. She had delicate, coffee cup sized breasts, a round, child-like face. Her hair was loose and fell about her shoulders. There was a bright gold ring in her nose. She looked to be all of eighteen or nineteen years old. Her hands were resting on her hips behind her back and her eyes were downcast. Her thighs were spread wide and Jake could see a little tuft of brown hair above her otherwise naked, puffy sex. She bore a red and black tattoo of a fearsome looking bear on her belly. She also bore the tell-tale Cyrillic writing across her upper chest denoting her slave name.

How could he blame Burnham for becoming enamored of the lifestyle here while he was strupping daily, as often as he could, a young woman who he now considered his property? This whole thing was going all wrong. How many crimes would they have to commit to save one girl?

What made her so special that they should inflict so much suffering on other young women just as innocent as she in order to save her? But he had taken a contract. He had never quit a job until it was finished. He looked at the brown haired slave girl. She would be a slave whether they were here or not. What difference did it really make?

Jake let the issue go. And he relented with regard to Klara, letting Burnham have her for four full days before she was returned. She looked at him darkly and, for the first time, he whipped her for her insolence. He was depressed for two days afterwards, berating himself for his cruelty. On the evening of the second day he called Klara to him. He had not touched her since he had beaten her. She knelt obediently before him in his room, naked and subservient. When she saw the whip that he held, she shivered in fear.

Jake stepped up to her and lifted her chin with one hand, holding the whip in another. He looked into her frightened, doleful eyes. He showed her the whip and threw it into the corner of the room. "*Niemals,*" he said, a German word he knew that he hoped was close enough to the Dutch equivalent for her to understand. He saw that she did understand it and her normal, toneless, blank demeanor collapsed. She began to cry and bent over to kiss his feet. "*Dank! Dank!*" she blurted out. "*Dank!*"

The next day Jake and Irkut were on the road again. Jake brought Klara with them but he insisted that she remain unhooded. And he convinced Burnham to let him bring another slave girl for Irkut so he wouldn't have to share his possession.

Two weeks later they were at their fifth estate. Jake had inspected all of the yearlings that he could find although their search had only covered the northern tier of pony girl estates. There were at least fifteen or twenty others that they hadn't visited yet. Jake and Irkut were standing at a white rail fence watching yet another female, fresh to her bit, run frantically around the track for their benefit. The pony master stood next to them, his heavily booted foot on the bottom rail. "You sure you're only interested in yearlings?" he asked. The other two yearlings that Jake and Irkut had watched perform were standing tethered to the fence some distance away, out of earshot, red neoprene hoods covering their features, nervously stepping from foot to foot in the dirt.

"My employer is looking to develop a young stable," Jake answered. "He's willing to spend some time to build a competitive estate team in a couple of years. We've got some good trainers who like to start from scratch."

"Okay, okay," the pony master said. "But this one here's the fastest of the three. I won't tell you that she doesn't need a lot of work. But she has potential. A year or two of muscle building and the right training she could be a good four pony team horse. Pull a cabriolet or maybe a brougham."

Irkut looked at Jake and shrugged his shoulders. He had guessed long ago that this pony girl search was more than it seemed. But what business of it was his? Let the *Americanskis* spend their money. "Not bad," he said.

They later settled on the third pony for 25,000 euros. Afterwards, they sat on the porch of the large mansion sipping cool, estate brewed beer. The owner had joined them. The conversation, as it usually did, turned to the pony races.

"We've got a good team," the owner said. "But our nine pony landau is our best. They're running third overall now and I think we have a shot at a medal at the finals."

"Congratulations," Jake said, feigning interest.

"But I understand that you're interested in yearlings."

Jake nodded getting ready to tell his bullshit story for the umpteenth time.

"Well, you should hang around for our races on Saturday. There's a yearling running then that's tearing up the track."

This piqued Jake's interest. Any chance to get a look at a couple of more yearlings was worth the wait.

"The thing is," the estate owner continued, "she's not running as a yearling. She's been moved up to sulky class. Won her last three races. Ours is probably no match for her, but it'll be fun watching her run."

* * * * * * * * * * * *

Maddy had, in fact, won her last three races. She had lost two after her first win and had suffered for it dearly. She had grown to hate with a special passion the four foot tall demon who was her master. The only oasis that existed for her in his world of whips and confinements was when she won a race. And then only on the actual day of the race. By the next morning, she would be back to the tortuous training routine, back to sexual deprivation.

And so Maddy looked forward to race day. She could earn temporary surcease from hell if she won and she couldn't win if there was no race. The Grobgy caravan arrived late Friday afternoon. Maddy was cleaned by the oppressively morose, black haired slave girl, fed, watered and allowed to pee. She was then locked in her little home away from home, the four by four steel cage. Maddy actually didn't mind much. If she couldn't have the delightful freedom and comfort provided by her former driver, she would take darkness. The tarp that covered her cage each time she was locked inside it blocked out the terrors of her new existence, allowed her to recall in her mind the pleasures that had been her small compensation for being dehumanized.

She no longer feared being returned to the pony barn at the end of the season. Life there was so much better than life under the dwarf. And if her former trainer was waiting to heap abuse on her when she returned, she would take it as a punishment for her foolish belief that he had felt something for her.

That night, the ponies were displayed in a wide circle on the front lawn of the estate mansion. It was a tradition to have a party each night before a 'home' race and to display the ponies that would run the next day for the benefit of the party goers. So Maddy stood, her neck affixed to a pole, her legs spread and attached to rings in the ground, while well dressed, jovial and curious members of the local elite took their turn to admire the fine ponyflesh.

It was typical to have a placard at the feet of the ponygirl which denoted her age, in pony years, and her nation of origin. The mostly Russian ruling class of Kalikastan took great pleasure in dehumanizing American, German and English females, a remnant of past wars, hot and cold. Other nations were represented, of course, for example, Poland, Romania, Italy, Spain and the Scandinavian countries.

Maddy's placard indicated her status as a yearling and her American origin. A special note remarked that she was running the 1500 meter sulky. Word had gotten around about the speedy yearling and she attracted much attention. Guests were supposed to look, but not touch, but quite a few of the revelers felt it appropriate to massage her large, round breasts or stroke her thighs. Only one man had the nerve to actually place his fingers on her hairless and exposed sex. Dressed in a finely tailored tuxedo, he rubbed the ponygirl until she moaned and then he stepped back laughing. He sniffed his hand and exchanged some no doubt witty words with his pretty, young companion, who was dressed in a flowing red gown with a bodice that hung from one shoulder and ran slanted, right to left across her chest. She carried a tall flute of champagne in her hand and giggled when the man spoke to her. She was tall and thin and her hair hung loose down her back. To Maddy she was ravishingly beautiful. But as far as she was concerned, that beauty hid a black heart if she could find humor in the dismal fate of what was once a fellow young woman.

Jake, not wanting to seem too anxious to take a peek at the ponies, downed a couple of gins while he strolled about the party. Everyone had him pegged as an American as soon as they saw him and most of the party goers shunned him. Only a tall brunette showed any real interest in him. He had told her that he was buying ponies for his American boss. She intimated that she would like to see his room. Jake demurred since he had seen the guy that the shapely, young woman had come in with. He was four feet wide and looked as mean as a crocodile. The brunette smiled and wandered away.

About an hour into the party, Jake strolled leisurely out to the lawn where the ponies were posted. He held his gin on the rocks in his left hand and navigated a Lucky Strike in his right back and forth to his mouth. He took time perusing the pony flesh. He had seen all of the home estate's ponies over the three days that they had stayed there. He had actually gotten to drive one of the non-racing teams, two buxom, broad backed females, former racers who had found a niche in providing pleasurable rides through the countryside bordering the estate for the master and his guests. He hardly had to touch the reins, the ponies knew the route so well.

And so Jake concentrated on examining the Grobgy team. He stepped quickly past the older ponies. When he came upon the yearlings, he examined them closely. They both had long, brown hair, but the one seemed a mite too tall to be Maddy. Both of their young bodies were perfect down to the delicate lips that bordered their pleasure holes. Neither had the tell-tale mole over the left hip that he had seen in the picture of Maddy. He walked on to the other ponies, examining them cursorily. He wanted to see the yearling that had graduated to sulky class. Nothing in Maddy's past, except her long legs and thick build, indicated that she would be any kind of racing phenomenon, so he had his doubts that he would find her. He looked down and saw the sign first. '*Molnya*', whatever that meant. '*Americanski*'. That piqued his interest. He looked up and saw the well lit form of the ponygirl. Her head was featureless, of course, covered by her blue and gold racing hood. And her mouth was covered by a broad leather shield that formed part of the thick leather gag that she wore in her mouth. He could not see her eyes, hidden behind the tiny holes that gave her extremely limited vision, just enough to see the track ahead while she raced.

She had fine, ample breasts with dark wide areolas. Her stomach was trim and firm, her legs long and, although thickly muscled, graceful. She wore the angry, yellow, rampant wolf etched on her belly with her estate's motto, '*Sub Hoc Signo Vinces*' – 'Under This Sign We Shall Conquer', in florid, blue lettering, underneath it. Her spread legs revealed the small, golden disks that were suspended from the bottom of her nether lips and they sparkled in the bright flood lights that shined down around the displayed ponies. He then raised his eyes to her hip.

There it was! The mole! Jake's heart leaped. Could it really be her? She was the right size. Her breasts were a little smaller, and she was a little thinner than in the picture, but that could be due to the intense training she had gone through. Jake remembered the laughing picture of the somewhat younger Maddy he had taken from her apartment. Was this that seemingly carefree girl? Did she have any humanity left? How long could a woman live the life of a beast without becoming one?

He decided on a test. Two well dressed couples had joined him and he knew that he had to be careful. If word got out that he and Burnham had faked their way into the country to rescue a ponygirl, they would be skinned and tarred. And that would just be preliminaries. And there were his people too: Leon and Curley, Martinez and Tucker, all good men, all willing to brave dangers at his command. They were all housed at Burnham's estate enjoying the local enslaved talent. But they would get quite a surprise if their cover were blown.

Jake leaned forwards slightly and whispered in a low, barely audible voice, "Maddy."

Maddy had noticed the short, fit man watching her. He seemed to have an inordinate interest in her flesh. She did not care, she had nothing to hide, she was used to it. She was proud of her trim, fit body, even if it was presented in the guise of an animal. It would have been different if her face had been displayed. What was normally such a burden and source of unhappiness to her served as a protective shield on the nights when the ponygirls were displayed to the gawking public. She was glad she was anonymous, showed no personality. She didn't have to hide her head in shame. It was already hidden. No one she had ever known would recognize her like this.

Then the she heard it. It was almost like a sigh of the leaves of the tall oak trees that hovered above them. Maybe it was a sound from the party going on in the house, because she could hear laughter and song and music coming from there. Her head and body jerked as soon as she heard it. The man who had been watching her had turned his back and was walking away. Could he have said it? But how could he? How could he know her? And what could he do, would he do, to help her?

One of the men from the two couples that had been standing next to Jake was leaning over and placed his hand on Maddy's right breast, tweaking the nipple. Maddy turned her head to the man and screamed and moaned in her gag, tugging and yanking at her bonds. All it took was that slight, probably imagined, reminder of who she once had been to set her off. She roared and pulled at the chain that connected her collar to the pole behind her. Her breasts shook and flowed east to west as her body convulsed. The man stepped back, alarmed. One of the grooms came running up and urged the two couples away. He then gave Maddy two sharp lashes across her breasts with the short whip that he held in his hand. It was enough to sting, but not mark, the skin.

The pain at her breasts cleared her head and calmed her down. The man who had spoken, if he had spoken, was already back in the house. Pretty, well dressed couples still strolled the walkway amidst the ponygirls. She could hear the pseudo-rock music from the party. She was naked, hooded and bound. Everything was as it was. Nothing had changed. She was a ponygirl, a beast of burden, but a valuable one. She would race tomorrow and win. That was all that mattered. Her prior life was dead.

Jerzi beat Lightning severely when he heard about her misbehavior at the pony paddock. But just on her belly and breasts.

In the morning, Lightning had an easy time of it. Although the disconcerting fantasy she had had the night before still haunted her, she was able to bear down and win the race handily. She received her normal reward of a multiorgasmic fucking by her driver afterwards and then they packed up and headed for the next race.

Jake had watched from the grandstands. He was amazed at Maddy's strength and agility. She was definitely a crowd favorite as it cheered her wildly during the pony parade before the race. Maddy had looked splendid, bedecked in her blue and gold finery, prancing with her knees high, her body straight and her breasts bouncing enticingly as she passed the reviewing stand. She was a fine specimen of a ponygirl. He had seen a lot over the last few weeks and she was heads above the rest. But her value as a ponygirl would make rescuing her all that much harder. He was sure that her owner would leave no stone unturned if she was stolen and the country would be sealed off as tight as a condom. He and Burnham needed to talk.

CHAPTER SIX
THE PONY GIRL TOURNAMENT

In an inn several miles from the Grobgy estate, Anton Drabik lay in a large, soft bed next to the beautiful and usually haughty daughter of his boss. Anya Grobgy was tall and curvaceous, young and beautiful. She was the apple of her father's eye and knew that his protective nature would not approve of her fucking his principal assassin. In fact, although she lived in a world where the fucking of women and former women was an everyday, every hour affair, much of it performed in public, Grobgy strictly forbade the violation of his daughter's chastity, at least as far as men went. He knew that she took her turns with the slave girls almost every night and that she once in a while availed herself of the pretty, shapely flesh of a ponygirl. But that was different.

And so Anya's and Drabik's torrid affair was a secret, or so they thought. Actually, Grobgy knew all about it. He hadn't quite decided whether to have his main trigger man zapped or to announce their engagement. He could do worse in a son-in-law, he thought. And who would protect his daughter when he was gone, for sooner or later, he knew, someone would put a bullet in him.

But he didn't know that Drabik and Anya were into fun and games. It had started innocently enough. While watching Drabik assault and fuck the ponygirl Lightning at her request, Anya had dared Drabik to "fuck me like a ponygirl". At their next tryst, Drabik had taken the initiative and tied her to the bed, fucking her throat as if it belonged to one of his hooded, former human charges. At first Anya had protested and she had choked and squealed when Drabik had thrust his cock down her throat. Her arms and legs were tied off with tight, thin cords and she could not oppose Drabik's desires. Afterwards, she was effusive in her excitement. She had never been fucked like that. Never. Drabik's surprise took on a life of its own.

Their routine was first to take the edge off of their fierce desire for each other's flesh with a wild, passionate fuck. Now was the interlude. Anya had her hand on Drabik's flaccid cock, caressing it gently, patiently awaiting its revival. Drabik was laying back thinking of his former charge, Lightning. There were two more weeks to the championship tournament. Then she would be back. With or without a trophy, he desired her. More than the flesh of this stuck up cunt next to him. She was a passionate bitch and it was fun to fuck her right under her father's nose, but nothing compared with looking down at a hooded head, its mouth encompassing your cock and knowing that you could do anything you wanted.

As his cock began to stiffen, Drabik thought that it was time to take the next step in their games. He had bound Anya tightly to the bed many times now, and even shoved a ring gag into her mouth to force her to mouth fuck. But he wanted to get her nearer to the ideal female and he figured it was time to stretch the envelope this time.

"Wait till you see what I've got for you," Drabik said to Anya as he rolled from the bed and retrieved his bag. He zipped it open and produced a ponygirl collar. "For your next lesson in fucking like a ponygirl, Anya. Come here and let me put this on you. "

Anya wasn't sure. The bondage thing excited her; her powerlessness at resisting Drabik's rock hard, fat cock made her blood hot. But a collar? Suppose she couldn't get it off.

"Oh, don't look at me that way," Drabik chided her. "Come here. You'll love it."

Despite her qualms, Anya's pussy began to tingle at the thought of being trussed like a ponygirl. As long as it was play. No one would want the actual life of a ponygirl. No one. But to play at it was fun.

Anya turned her back to Drabik and he lifted the hair from the back of her neck. "Here, hold this," he instructed her. Anya received the bunched hair from his hands. Drabik opened the collar and placed it around Anya's neck. The pony collars were a combination of leather and hard plastic. It was about three inches wide at the back and seven inches at the front. The collars had a little dip in the front to accommodate the chin and the result was to hold the ponygirl's head in a slightly upwards position. When a ponygirl leaned forward during a race in an effort to move the heavy burden behind her, her head was in a perfect position to view the track ahead. The collar had a long, broad strap in the back that was used to affix the ponygirl's wrists. The wrists were tied off low in the back, just above the buttocks so that there would be little pressure on the neck. Most new ponygirls did not experience discomfort to their arms in this pose. Some of the less limber ones felt the tension in their shoulders for a few days, but that soon went away as the muscles stretched to accommodate their new, permanent positioning.

Drabik locked the collar snugly around Anya's throat. Her hands went up to it, feeling its soft leather stretched over its hard plastic form. "I want to see myself," she said, and she rushed over to the mirror on the wall. It was a full length mirror and she could see her curvaceous, naked body, her heavy black thatch that surrounded her sex. She saw her graceful, almost perfect facial features in it now framed by the pony collar. She gripped the edges of the collar, her eyes wild with amazement and delight. "Oh, Anton," she said, her eyes glued to her strange looking form, "it feels so overwhelming. I can't move my head. I have to move my whole shoulders, see?"

Anya turned her shoulders at her lover. He was admiring the way it tilted her head up in that familiar way. He stepped forward so that he could affix her wrists to the strap that hung down her back. She felt him lean against her back and saw his scarred face in the mirror over her shoulder. "You look lovely, Anya," he told her. "Just one more thing."

Anya's cunt began to cream as she felt Drabik lift her wrists behind her back. By the time he had both wrists bound, her heart was beating wildly. "Oh, Anton," she said once again.

Drabik ran his hands down Anya's chest and belly from behind. Anya watched the hands in the mirror. She thrust her plump, white breasts at them, sighing with pleasure as he teased her hard nipples. She spread her legs willingly as the hands reached her enflamed sex. She gasped when the fingers of one hand drew her engorged nether lips apart and slid inside her lubricated gash. While the one hand explored the depths of her cunt, the other worried the little bud at its top. "Ahhhhhhhhh!" Anya moaned as the tremors of her pleasure flowed through her. Drabik dragged the bound, black haired beauty over to the end of the bed and pushed her torso over the footboard. He kicked her legs apart.

"This is how a ponygirl gets it Anya," he told the deliriously lustful woman. The assassin cum ponygirl trainer reached down to Anya's flooded pussy and gathered her moisture on the fingers of his right hand. He spread it over and inside of her dainty brown flower between her upturned rear cheeks.

"Oh, no Anton, not there please," Anya moaned as she struggled weakly to get up. She had never let anyone breach that portal.

"Ponygirls don't get to decide where they're fucked, Anya," Drabik replied as he pried the rear hole wider with his fingers. As he did so, with his other hand, he guided his rigid tool to Anya's sex. He probed the opening and sank right in.

"Ohhhhhhhhhh!" Anya moaned as she felt him fill her. This was what she wanted. Her pussy burned with need.

"Don't get too excited, Anya," the course, cruel man told her. "I'm just getting myself all lubed up."

Drabik ran his cock back and forth in the depths of Anya's sheath. Her breathing became deep and her thighs began to tremble. She was ready to come. Suddenly, her shaft was empty. The fingers no longer probed at the tight ring of her ass. Instead, she felt the head of Drabik's prick seeking entry.

"Please don't, Anton, please!" she moaned. "Oh, it hurts, please don't!" Again she struggled to lift her torso from the bed, but Drabik's hand pressed firmly into her back, pinning her to the bed.

Drabik had been pushing his cock past the tight ring surrounding the entrance to Anya's bowels. He gave a sigh as he sank deeper, feeling the warmth of her innards surround his cock. The pretty gangster's daughter whined as she felt the delicate tissue of her anal ring rend.

"It only hurts till you get used to it, Anya," he told her. "Ponygirls have no choice. In fact, in my experience, they love to ass fuck. You'll get to love it too, I sure," he said, taunting the supine, moaning woman. Slowly, he sank himself to the hilt inside her. And then slowly he began to rasp his hard, fat cock over the stretched and torn ring of Anya's brown star. He reached below her with his other hand and began to softly stroke her hardened pleasure bud. The effect on the young woman was electrifying. Her body began to shudder and she began to cry out, "Ah! Ah! Ah! Ah! Ah!" as her first orgasm overcame her. She had orgasmed before, many, many times. But this one was different. All the others were like beer compared to champagne. Her ass was filled to burst and the sensation sent a stupefying thrill through her.

Drabik maintained his steady stroke in Anya's ass. He continued to tease her stiff clit and soon had her moaning and crying out in ultimate passion once again. After the second orgasm, he removed his hand. Placing his hands on her rear globes, he began to fuck her ass in earnest, driving back and forth, pounding the front of his thighs into hers. Anya started to blubber and cry as yet another orgasm tore through her. Her bound wrists churned behind her back; she could feel the heavy collar around her neck. She was imprisoned and yet free, free to let her sexual energy pour out of her unrestrained, but powerless to regulate the use of her own body. Finally, almost gratefully, she heard her lover's heavy, deep groan and felt his hot load shoot into her. She came again, writhing and moaning, all the time drilling into her mind a single mantra, "Fucking was never like this! Fucking was never like this! Fucking was never like this!"

* * * * * * * * * * * * * * * * *

Jake had phoned Burnham right away and given the verbal signal that he had found Maddy. His boss had a hard time disguising his glee. Although Jake wanted to go back to the estate and begin planning Maddy's rescue, he didn't want to do anything to clue in Irkut that something odd was going on. They had three more estates to visit.

Jake sleepwalked through the next few days. He treated Klara curtly. She sensed his discordant mood and tried desperately to please him. She knew that even though he had promised not to whip her, that is, if she understood him correctly, he could always change his mind or give her to somebody who would. Although the former Dutch citizen hated and despised her condition of servitude, he was not the worst of the men who she had been forced to pleasure and he sometimes could be nice.

Jake had gone directly to Burnham when he arrived back at the estate. He found him in a conference room he had built talking things over with some shady local types. Everyone was smiling and so they probably had just closed a deal.

"Hey, Jake, good work. We'll talk in a minute. This is Arcady Renko and his brother Ilya. We're going to be partners in a new endeavor."

Jake looked at the men suspiciously. "What's that?" he asked his employer.

"I'm opening my own training facility. These fellows are going to run it."

"What?" Jake asked, taken aback at the startling revelation. "You're going to train slave girls?"

"Sure, why not," Burnham answered.

"Because...," he paused and looked at the expectant faces of the two slavers. He wanted to remind Burnham that it was wrong. That it was cruel. That it was bad for his soul. But he dared not speak of one of the most cherished local institutions that way.

"The Commission..." he started to say.

"I've already got clearance from the Commission. There's going to be a big need for slave girls when the pipeline construction begins in earnest. We expect 15 to 20,000 workers for three years. That'll require a boatload of pussy."

"Won't the local competitors object? You're breaking their monopoly." Jake knew already that Burnham had taken care of this. He was a dynamic man, but cautious.

"There'll be plenty of wealth to go around," Burnham responded. His attention was directed at several sheets of colorful drawings on the table. "Which one of these do you like?" Burnham asked him, disregarding Jake's obviously disapproving tone.

"What do you mean?" Jake asked. The drawings looked like pen and ink drawings of animal heads and such. Then he realized what he was looking at. If Burnham was starting a slave training center, he would need a distinctive trade mark. One his 'products' would wear tattooed on their bellies.

"I don't really think I'm in a position to….."

"Of course you are, Jake." Burnham said, interrupting him impatiently. He looked up from the table for the first time and stared Jake in the eyes. "I've fucked that little cunny you own, which you got on my dime by the way," he said. "And I'm sure she wasn't acting as a local guide on your recent trip. So don't get all high and holy with me, Jake. Okay?"

Jake looked at Burnham resignedly. Of course he was right. And the only way Jake could put a stop to Burnham's schemes was either to rat him out to Interpol, the State Department, the FBI, NATO, somebody, or kill him. But if he went to any law enforcement agency, his ass was grass too. Besides, he had never ratted in his life. And killing Burnham would not only ruin the mission but he would undoubtedly be wearing an earthen coat before he got a chance to go very far. No, he would go with the program.

"Okay," he said. "Let me see them."

Burnham handed Jake a pile of five or six sheets of paper, each with a finely drawn heraldic figure on it. One was a flexed Caucasian arm, fist closed, on an intense field of blue. Another was a bright red dragon, curled, its tail flaunted wildly, a stream of yellow flame emerging from its mouth.

"This is the one I like the best," Burnham said. He pointed to a drawing of the black head of a ferocious looking dog, a mastiff. Its red fangs were bared in an angry sneer. Its eyes were red too, adding to the beast's demonic mien.

Jake saw no reason to dissuade his employer. What difference did it make anyway? "Sure," he said. "That one looks good."

"It'll be the crest for my estate," Burnham informed him. "Here's the motto I've chosen," he said. On another sheet of heavy, white paper in fine script were the words, '*Vigilans et Audax*'. "It means 'Vigilance and Audacity'."

"Well, you're audacious," Jake told him ironically.

Burnham spent another fifteen minutes finishing his business with the Renko brothers. When they left Jake and Burnham finally got to talk.

"So how does she look?" Burnham asked.

"She looks like all the other ponygirls, Mr. Burnham. She was naked, hooded and tattooed."

"I mean physically, was she all right?"

"Mr. Burnham, she looked much better than all right. I'm sure that she's in the best shape she's ever been in her life. She's a world class pony girl. She'll be in the championships in two weeks. I saw her run. She's strong and fast."

Burnham smiled. "Who would've thought it," he said. "I guess I should be proud of her."

"Proud?" Jake asked, astonished at Burnham's reaction.

Burnham looked at Jake scornfully. "Of course, proud. She's prospered in adversity. Who can do better then that?"

"Mr. Burnham, she's living the life of an animal. She's probably been fucked by a hundred different men by now, maybe more. You've seen how they treat the ponygirls here."

"I've seen it Jake. You don't have to remind me that she's in dire straits. All I'm saying is that she's a survivor. It has to do with strength of character. Some girls would just crawl up in a ball and die. But she sounds like she's actually thriving."

Jake decided to not pursue the point further. "I can have a plan together for you in a day or so, Mr. Burnham. I can have my team ready by the championships. It's probably a great time to grab her since there'll undoubtedly be big crowds around, a lot of confusion."

Burnham reacted violently. "Absolutely not, Jake," he roared. "I've told you. I can't just let you go in like a gangbuster. It has to be done with subtlety. How do you think the people here would react if a highly competitive pony was snatched out right from under them? And at the championships too! You'll have to think of something better."

"Mr. Burnham, if you'll pardon the expression, you're putting the cart before the horse. We're not here to become lords of the manor or to become slavers. We're here to rescue Maddy."

"Jake, you're already a slaver. Your people in the States ship about five or six girls out here a week on average. That means that since we've been here, you're responsible for enslaving over a hundred pretty, young, innocent females. You own a slave. You've been buying slaves for me. You've been fucking them right and left for weeks. Just cut the shit. I'm not jeopardizing my operations. I want Maddy back but in a way that the locals can deal with. Once we have her, legitimately, we can smuggle her out, say she died or something. But we can't just snatch her."

Jake was furious. "And how will we get her 'legitimately'?" he asked irately.

"The way we get anything else we want," Burnham replied. "We'll buy her."

* * * * * * * * * * * * * *

The championships had finally arrived. Lightning had no concept of the championship, she just raced when she was told, slept when she was told and fucked or sucked when she was told. She had won two out of her last three races. She was getting better every day and if the season lasted another couple of weeks, there probably would have been no pony who could have matched her. She was swift and strong, but most of all she had a burning desire to win. Not just because of the beatings and abuse she suffered when she lost, not for the delight of the after win fuck that Jerzi condescended to give her, but because of an unquenchable desire to make herself real. She wanted to be remembered. She wanted to be an individual. And the only way she knew of under the circumstances to do that was to be the fastest pony on two legs.

When she was unloaded from the pony van after her arrival at the racing park where the championships were held, Lightning knew that something was different. Even from her dime sized little holes in her hood she could see that there were dozens of pony vans. She watched as ponies in red, green, black, brown and many other color hoods trotted by Jerzi's little encampment. Jerzi, himself, seemed to have a little spring in his step and he even once patted Lightning's flanks playfully. After she was unloaded, washed and fed, she was stored away in her little cage. With the dark tarp over it, she could not witness the frenetic activity as the teams of ponygirls arrived and assembled at their prearranged camp sites. But she could hear the rumble of van after van as they passed. She knew that something special was happening.

Later that afternoon, Lightning was taken out for a spin by her dwarfish driver. She emerged from a small copse of woods and saw the largest grandstand that she had seen so far. It was empty, but there were many teams of ponies coming and going. Jerzi wheeled her out onto the track and got her going at a trotting pace. He knew his business. Training was over. There would be no five mile heavy duty workouts. He just needed to ensure that his pony, Lightning, was kept supple and ready to race. He also wanted her to get used to the track and the flurry of activity. He didn't want her skittish or overwhelmed by her experiences to come.

He could, of course, have just told his pony that she was to compete in the championship, that if she failed him he would make her very, very sorry. After all, although she was no longer a human female, she probably retained some semblance of ability to understand language, even in the broken English that he had. But that would go against all of her training. If she thought that she was still a woman, she might despair at her condition and lie down and die. She might rebel and refuse to run. She might lose heart in the middle of a race. Besides, it would be cruel to unnecessarily remind her of her former humanity, and although he enjoyed laying the whip to her flesh and watching her squirm and moan in anguish, he didn't want to torment her mentally.

The championships were run, like the regular season races, in teams of two. Over the next two days, there would be eliminations. There were ten pony teams in each class selected, based on their weighted season scores, to compete in each divisional championship. It was double elimination until the semi and final rounds. The losers of the semi's battled it out for third place and a bronze medal. The winners battled for silver and gold.

That night there was a huge pony parade. It was opening night of the four day festival and people had come from all over the country, and some special guests from outside, to see the finest ponies in the world run. The grandstands were lit up like the Winter Palace on the Czar's birthday. There were colored lights and strings of pennants showing the heraldic symbols of all the pony estates. Grobgy's was up there, the rampant wolf, its paws raised to attack, its mouth snarling its anger and fierceness, the same that Lightning wore tattooed on her belly. It was mounted on blue and gold flags that had been set onto the carts of his racing teams. It was emblazoned on the blue and gold silk shirts that his drivers wore.

Each estate paraded together and so Lightning was able to see Persephone and her new cartmate ahead of her. She bristled a bit when she saw them but was cured of her unruliness by a fierce pull on her reins which drove her bridle deeply into her tongue. She quickly regained her step.

The first heats started early the next morning. Lightning had a middle seed, partly because of her predecessor, Starlight's record, and partly because of the four losses she had suffered. But it was better than bottom seed where the ponies had to compete against the best teams in the first round. After that, it was the luck of the draw and any team could find itself matched against the favorites.

Jerzi knew Lightning's abilities well and she cruised to victory in the first heat. She didn't get her usual reward since Jerzi wanted her on edge during the entire tournament. He let her suck his cock and then he jerked off into her mouth. That would have to do for a reward for now.

In her second heat, that afternoon, Lightning was up against one of the favorites. Jerzi cursed the luck of the draw. But he was a cagey and experienced ponygirl driver. Lightning might well be able to beat this pony, which had a 17 and 3 overall record. But she would tire herself out.

And then she might be beaten by even a mediocre team. Also, he didn't want the drivers of the really good ponies to know what she could do. If Lightning came up against the overall favorite before the finals, he wanted to surprise her driver, who would think that he had a cakewalk. Every edge would count.

And so Lightning lost her second round. Not by much, but enough so that the next pony that raced her might be eased off just a bit. He had to whip the unhappy pony, of course. He didn't want her to think that she didn't have to win. He could hear her crying and moaning as he laid the whip into her. Afterwards, he teased her hairless cunt until it was wet and hot and she moaned with need. Then he had her staked out at the rear of the pony van until she was needed for the next race.

She won the next race. It was a bit of a struggle and Lightning didn't have a clear lead until coming around the home turn. But she won and her racing was over for the day.

Jake and Burnham had watched Maddy run from the grandstands. There was desultory betting on the qualifiers and a small crowd had turned out. In other sections of the fairgrounds there was food and music and even pony rides. For fifteen zlotskis you and your girl could take a spin around the park in a nine pony landau. Or you could watch the show pony exhibition where the ponies had been trained to prance and canter, wheel and strut. There was even a slave girl brothel where an ordinary guy could get a taste of finely trained pussy. Over the four days of the festival there was always a line.

Lightning slept fitfully. She knew by now that this was some kind of championship. That so many people could devote so much energy and resources to this cruel sport amazed her. It drove home to her the futility of any hope of return to former days.

Her first race in the morning was a tough one, tougher than Jerzi would have wanted. Lightning won by a head and she had used up considerable energy. There were two more races that day. If Lightning won them both, she would be in the semis. The semi's were held in the morning of the fourth day of the tournament with the finals in the afternoon. There were three different ponies that Lightning could draw as her opponents. Two of them were tough, with high seeds. The third was an over achiever who was due for a fall. Lightning drew the overachiever first and defeated her convincingly. Next, worst luck, she drew the overall favorite.

Isabella, once called Maria Delgado, was a tall, strong Andalusian from the hilly, rocky coast of southern Spain. Her skin was deep brown, almost russet, and her hair was a shiny, deep black. She had fine, large breasts, as any good ponygirl would, and solid, trunk like thighs. Like all of the premier ponygirls, she was shapely and her torso was sleek. She was a three year old and was last year's spring and fall champion. She had lost once all season and had not lost yet in the tournament.

Perhaps it was her fiery Moorish temperament or the circumstances that surrounded her capture and dehumanization that made her tough and mean. She had been a college student in Madrid when she got a call from her father to come home right away, that he was sick and needed to see her. Her father was a drunken fool who had gambled all of the family's money away. She despised him, but family was family, and she left immediately to go see him. She received a cell phone call from him for her to meet him near the docks. The address that he gave her was a small, run down warehouse. When she stepped in the door, a black bag was pulled over her head and her arms were joined together in a vice-like grip. She heard her father begging and pleading and then felt a jab in her arm.

She didn't have time to scream. In a moment, she was unconscious. That was the last she saw of Spain.

The second day of races, the third day of the festival, drew a larger crowd than the day before. The contenders had been thinned out and there were some real, meaningful races going on. If she lost, Lightning was out of the tournament. There was always next year, but that's what losers always say. Jerzi believed that she could do it, but only if she followed his lead with iron discipline.

Jake and Burnham were back in the stands. Burnham watched with his binoculars as his niece was led up to the starting line. He had a program in his hand. "This one is unbeaten," he told Jake, referring to Maddy's opponent. They had watched all of Maddy's races. Jake had to admit that the excitement of the races was contagious, but Burnham was taking a more than idle interest in it. After all, he had racing ponies of his own. Burnham put down his glasses while waiting for the 'ready' horn. "Here," he said.

Jake looked down. It was a betting ticket. He couldn't read the writing, but he guessed what pony's name was on it. "You bet on your niece?" he asked, incredulous.

"Ten grand," Burnham said. "It's 2 ½ to 1. Good odds. That's 25,000. Euros, not dollars."

"Jesus wept, Mr. Burnham. How far are you going to take this?"

"That's your bonus, Jake. For finding Maddy. If she wins you've got a good piece of change. If she loses, you got shit. So you better get on your feet and cheer for her." He lifted up his binoculars and zoomed in on the two ponies, side by side. The ready horn sounded and the two ponies poised to spring from their starting positions, their lead feet deeply planted in the dirt of the track, their back toe poised to advance. The gun sounded and they were off.

Jerzi's strategy was simple. He didn't want to go wire to wire with the former champion. He didn't want to fall too far behind. So he kept Lightning's head even with Isabella's left wheel. Isabella, as the higher seed, had the outside post.

Lightning wondered what was going on. She knew that she could run faster than this, but her driver kept the reins tight, easing her head back when she went too quickly. Did he want her to fail so he could beat her? No, she decided, he could beat her anytime he wanted. He was the driver. She was the pony. He knew more than she did. She would follow his lead as if it was the word of God.

Isabella, like Lightning, had already worked hard today. Her driver wanted her to save her stuff until tomorrow. She was guaranteed a spot in the semi's already, but he wanted her record to be perfect. He wanted his pony to be at her most confident when she attempted to repeat as Spring Champion. So he eased off, letting the other pony, the upstart yearling, run out of steam. At the half mark, Jerzi let Lightning go a little faster. When he sped up, Isabella sped up. He would make Lightning fall behind and then Isabella would slow. He did this three times. When they passed the ¾ turn he did it again. But this time, when Isabella slowed, he jerked Lighting's reins hard and cracked her back viscously with the whip. "Hiyaaaah!" he called to her. Lightning needed no other encouragement; she dug her toes in hard and gave her driver all that she had.

Burnham had been moaning and groaning throughout the race. "What's that driver doing?" he asked no one in particular. "Jesus Christ! She can do better than that!" He shouted out to the driver who most certainly could not hear him, "You fucking bum!"

Jake too was taken up with the excitement of the race. Maddy, he had realized from the crowd's reactions to her, was the sentimental favorite. Her adversary was the best pony around at this class. The crowd was jammed up against the rail, pressed up against the glass of the clubhouse. Jake and Burnham were on the edge of their seats in the stands. "Come on, Maddy! Come on!" Burnham yelled. Jake looked around to see if anyone had noticed. He had told Burnham a dozen times that her pony name was 'Lightning'.

He had just raised his binoculars again to see how Burnham's niece was doing when Jake saw the driver yank the reins and Maddy leap into full speed. He and Burnham both stood up as did everyone in the stands. "Look! Look!" Jake yelled. "She's pulling ahead!"

She was pulling ahead. The trick was to make your move close enough to the finish line so that your advantage of surprise would last. But you didn't want to wait until you got into the home stretch because the other driver would pour it on once the finish line was in view. Jerzi had done it just right. Lightning was a full length away before Isabella's driver could recover. Isabella was slowing down, not speeding up, and her trend had to be reversed. He was astounded at Lightning's burst of speed. What had begun as a cakewalk was now a real race.

It made matters worse that once Jerzi had achieved a full cart length ahead of the other team, he pulled out a few feet from the rail. Now the other pony had to move further to the outside and then try to catch him. He had studied Isabella well. He knew that she almost never ran from behind and he was gambling that she would not know how to put on the extra effort to draw back ahead until they had crossed the finish line.

Lightning could see the bright yellow tape of the finish line looming ahead as they hit the stretch. She didn't know that she was facing elimination; she didn't know that she was racing the holder of the course record. All she knew was that she was ahead and meant to stay that way. She pounded her feet into the track, drawing every ounce of strength from her legs, kicking them high. Her chest felt like to burst as she drew great drafts of air inside her aching lungs. She was thirty meters away, twenty meters away. Just then the other pony peeked her head slightly ahead of hers. Isabella, like the champion that she was, had made up the ground that she had lost and was about to pull ahead. With a final, Herculean push, Lightning regained the lead just as they crossed the finish line. The yellow tape draped around her head and neck as proof of her victory. The crowd was roaring loudly. She could barely hear them over the mighty beating of her heart, the rushing of blood in her ears. They had just seen the best race of the day, if not of the tournament. The upstart yearling had beaten the champ!

* * * * * * * * * * * * * *

Jake and Burnham spent the night in the large, luxurious camper that the multi-millionaire had brought. A vast campground had been set up for festival visitors and the tents and campers stretched for hundreds of meters. After Maddy's last race of the day, they decided to take in the sights. Burnham said that he had some business to conduct. There was a large tent set up near the ponygirl encampment where some estates were selling off ponygirls for one reason or another. These were clearly not first class ponies and were mainly for the aftermarket, wealthy 'new men' not rich enough to own their own estates, carnival operators, and even breeders. Kalikastan issued very few export licenses for ponygirls, for obvious reasons, but they did issue a few and you could usually see a few dark skinned, robed Arabs perusing the goods.

Burnham wanted to pick up a good dray team, for hauling things around his estate and for afternoon rides in the country. They had to be big and strong for two of them to pull a cart with a heavy man like Burnham in the driver's seat. A couple of the larger nine and six pony teams had been broken up and there were a few ponies to choose from.

The huge tent was divided into several stalls. Each stall had its own dealer and selection of pony stock. Jake and Burnham took their time checking them out. Ultimately, Burnham selected a pair of light skinned blondes. They were former teammates and their seller insisted that they would run well together as a two pony team. Burnham handled their thighs and backs. Their bits were removed and he examined their mouths and their teeth. Both of the ponies sported a snarling tiger's head on their bellies. They wore black hoods and their eye holes were covered, blinding them. Ponygirls had no need to see who was buying them. They were standing with their necks affixed to a horizontal pole by a short chain that led to the back of their collars. They stood shoulder to shoulder with the other 8 ponygirls this dealer had for sale.

"What are their names," Burnham asked the dealer once he satisfied himself that he spoke a passable form of English. He was a rough sort of fellow with what looked like three day old whiskers and a dirty, dark green t-shirt and blue jeans. He was surprised to meet the famous American ponygirl owner. He picked him out right away. So much for discretion.

"Good afternoon Mr. Burnham. I have been to Chicago," he said in his Slavic accent. "The Cobs, baseball. I like it a lot." Burnham just smiled and nodded.

"This one is Flora and the other one is Dora," the second hand pony dealer said, apparently disappointed that

Burnham was not a Chicago Cubs fan. "But you can call them anything you want."

Jake was surprised when he saw Burnham slide his hand between Dora's thighs. Dora, obediently spread her legs and accommodated him.

"She's hot," the dealer told Burnham. "They both are. Go ahead, make her come."

It didn't take long for Dora's gash to begin to lubricate. She had heavy breasts and long, thin nipples. She had broad shoulders and stood taller than Jake. Jake could not resist the temptation to reach out and fondle one of her breasts. She sighed as he cupped it.

Satisfied that Dora was responsive enough to serve as a beast of burden and comely and passionate enough to serve as a sometimes fucktoy, Burnham tested Flora's responses as well. She began to pant almost at once and Jake could see her breasts rise and her nipples stiffen. While she was a little smaller than Dora, her breasts were similar in size. A classic matched pair. "I'll give you 35,000 euros for them both," Burnham told the dealer. "But I need certified papers." The second hand market for slave girls and ponies was strictly regulated. Theft was a major problem.

"Don't worry about papers," the scurvy man said. "I get you papers. But 35,000 euros? I piss on that. €35,000 each perhaps."

Burnham hated being overcharged, as did most multi-millionaires. That's how he got his money to start with.

"Look," Burnham told the man, "these ponies are at least seven years old. Look at the marks by their bits and the feel the grooves on their shoulders from the harness. And these muscles are tired. They won't last another two years. "I'll give you €40,000 for both.

Jake wondered where Burnham got his knowledge about ponygirls. He must have been putting more time into it than he thought.

"No way, *Amerikanski*," the man said. "You are insulting me. They have mouth watering tits and graceful, sweet hips. I cannot part with them for less than €65,000 for both."

"Let's go Jake," Burnham said.

The dealer looked shocked. "You don't want to buy them?"

"Not at these prices," Burnham told him.

"Wait, wait," the dealer said. "Okay. Okay. You are new to my country, just starting out. I tell you what I do; I give you both for €55,000."

Burnham paused. He looked at the pair of tall, bulky blondes again. "€45,000 and it's a deal."

There was silence. The dealer was thinking, probably calculating his profits and subtracting the cost of feeding and housing them until he could find another buyer. Suddenly, he spoke again. "Okay. Okay. You are robbing me, but it's a deal." Burnham and the man shook hands. "Of course there's a delivery charge of 200 euros." The dealer added.

"Don't need it," Burnham replied. "I've got a van."

Jake looked at him, surprised.

Burnham looked back. "I bought it yesterday. Figured I'd need it."

Burnham had two 20 thousand euro drafts from a Dlitski bank with him. The rest he would pay in cash. The dealer looked at them and flipped open his cell phone. He chattered into it rapidly, looking at the papers. After a few minutes of animated conversation, he flipped the telephone closed.

He looked nervous. "Your drafts are no good, Mr. Burnham," he said.

"What!" Burnham yelled. "That's bullshit!"

"No, no, no, Mr. Burnham, you don't understand. You may have the ponies. A gift. From me. From my uncle."

In Kalikastan everyone referred to the leader of their clan as their uncle. It made it very confusing for outsiders, but the relationship was real. Clan loyalties ran deep.

"And who is your 'uncle'," Burnham asked.

"Oscar Kasperov," the dealer told him. "He would be honored if you took the ponies as his gift."

"With papers?" Burnham asked.

The dealer laughed. "Of course with papers!" he exclaimed, smiling. "Let's have a drink!"

A small table came out with folding chairs. Jake and Burnham and the dealer and a fellow who seemed to be his partner sat down. A skinny, brown skinned, naked slave girl with short black hair came rushing out with a tray with four glasses and a bottle of Vodka. She bowed to each of the men as she proffered them a glass. The dealer did the honors.

"To America!" he said, his glass held high. All the men tossed back their shots. Four more shots were poured.

"To Oscar Kasperov!" Burnham declared. The glasses were raised and emptied.

The dealer, his name still unknown, refilled the glasses again. He raised his glass.

The toasts went on for three more rounds. They toasted Kalikastan, the Cubs and ponygirls. Jake, finally, had to get up. "Jesus," he whispered to himself as the vodka hit home.

Burnham rose as well. "Tell Mr. Kasperov that I am honored to accept his gift and will be seeing him soon," Burnham told the dealer. "Please deliver the ponies to my trailer on the east side of the camping park. My estate flag flies above it.

"Oh yes, we know, the angry, mad dog." The dealer smiled. "A virile symbol."

"And a warning to others," Burnham added.

They took a last look at Burnham's new property. Jake wondered what Dora and Flora made of all this. Maybe they didn't care, he thought. Seven years a ponygirl. What could that be like? Burnham and Jake had gone about twenty yards when the dealer's partner came running after them. "Papers. Papers," he repeated as he handed two sealed documents to Burnham. Burnham smiled and put them in his pocket.

"Who's this guy Kasperov, Jake asked.

"The President of the National Commission and a partner," Burnham answered. And that was all he said. But Jake took note at how fast Burnham was rising in Kalikastani society.

They feasted and drank at the food booths and watched a fifteen girl troop of slave girls dance lasciviously for twenty five minutes. When Jake got back to the camper, he was randy and slightly drunk. The camper had two bedrooms and Klara was waiting for him in his. When he came in, she was kneeling on the bed, her head lowered and her hands parked behind her. Jake quickly disrobed and flung himself on the bed. "Suck my cock," he told her as he turned on his back.

The slave girl crawled between Jake's thighs and took his already hardening cock in her hands. She caressed it gently until it rose and then leaned over and took it between her lips. Her mouth and tongue created a soft suction and Jake sighed as the pleasurable warmth of his slave girl's mouth triggered a wave of relaxing sensation to flow through him. He closed his eyes and saw in his mind the multitude of pulchritude he had seen during the day: the bouncing breasts of the ponygirls as they dashed around the track, their bare lower lips enticingly available for all to see, their wide, sweet hips, the tautness of their decorated bellies. He had walked through the pony camp earlier in the day and tried to conger up the faces behind the hoods.

Without faces, they weren't human. It seemed natural to see them hitched to posts or rails, to watch as one or another was beaten for her failure to win.

Klara slowly moved her tight lips down the length of Jake's stiff manhood. He sighed again and placed his hand lazily upon her head in recognition and reward for her efforts. He felt her tongue swirling around the head of his prick, teasing the underside of its crown. She had his balls in her hand and was carefully, expertly squeezing them, coaxing them to produce their tart, white elixir.

Jake thought of Maddy, or Lightning, as she was called. She was beautiful. He recalled the short moments when he had examined her, leashed to a post, three weeks ago. Her fine breasts swayed gently as she almost unnoticeably shifted her weight from foot to foot. He imagined her for a moment, her plump lips surrounded by her neoprene head covering of blue, opened to receive him. At the same time, Klara took her broad, strong tongue and used it to stroke the length of his burning cock. She had loosened her long, straight, blond hair and he could feel it brush against his thighs and belly as she seized him again with her mouth. She forced her head down against his loins, her lips descending to the base of his cock. His meat entered her throat and the tightness sent a shiver through his body. She held it there until she heard Jake moan and then ascended the length of his pole, her broad lips dragging along the tight, sensitive skin.

In Jake's mind, it was Maddy sucking his cock. He thought of her long, toned legs and her pleasant, firm breasts. He imagined owning her, possessing her. This time, when Klara had implanted his throbbing rod in her throat, Jake felt his juices rising. He placed his other hand on the slave girl's head and moaned deeply. Klara, knowing the signal for what it was, began long rapid strokes of his cock with her mouth and throat. Jake's thighs tensed, his balls tightened. And then his whole body seemed to shudder as his prick exploded. Each spurt of cum sent a jolt through him. "Ohhhhhhhh!" he moaned as he felt himself pouring through his cock. "Ohhhhhhh!" Klara excited his instrument with her lips and tongue as he came, urging every drop of his seed from him.

When she felt his manhood begin to soften, Klara let the flaccid tool drop from her lips. Jake was breathing deep and regular. His mind had clouded after his orgasm and he felt himself drifting off. And then he remembered the blond slave girl who had brought his so much pleasure. He reached out and took her by the arm pulling her naked body up next to his. She flung her arm over his chest and pressed her breasts against his side. Jake fell asleep with his pretty slave girl nestled against him.

* * * * * * * * * * *

Lightning's night was not quite so interesting or tenderly restful. After her last race for the day, the black haired slave girl washed her and chained her to the rub down table. Jerzi came along and rubbed her back and leg muscles, working out the knots, encouraging the flow of blood within them. He teased Lightning's bare slit until he saw her moisture begin to ooze between her naked nether lips and then barked an order to the black haired girl. She released Lightning from the table, rehooked her wrists behind her back and pushed her to her knees. Jerzi came and stood in front of the ponygirl. Natasha, that was her name, Lightning had heard the dwarf yell it several times, knelt before him and trapped his thick, long cock between her lips. Lightning watched through her tiny eyeholes as the slave girl assiduously worked his member, stroking it with her hands, sheathing its length within her mouth.

Jerzi stood there, his eyes closed, his hands on his hips as he took his due from his slave.

Lightning knew what was coming. He did this almost every day. When he was ready, he pushed Natasha's head aside and stepped up to his pony. He released the bit that was still in her mouth and pushed the fat, round head of his cock inside her lips. Lightning stayed motionless. She did not have permission to seize the tiny man's prick with her lips, to give her lord and master pleasure. She waited, her lips apart, the thick cock laying on her tongue as the dwarf pulled at his meat, jerking at it rapidly until he groaned and Lightning felt the thick, white stream of his discharge flowing onto her tongue. She was the recipient of his spunk and nothing more. She was a tool to be used by him when and how he saw fit. Usually, after a victorious race, she would have earned the right to take pleasure from him, to grunt and moan on her back while he plowed her hot channel. But not this time. It was his signal to her that her task was not done. That there were more races to run. That she would have to prove herself worthy one or more times again the next day.

Lightning received Jerzi's spunk dutifully. When he pulled the head of his drooling meat from her lips, she opened her mouth wide and showed him the product of his lust. He zipped his pants and walked away, her signal to swallow.

After the slaver girl fed her, Lightning spent her evening in her little cage. The she was watered and allowed to pee and blinded and bound for the night, lying stretched out on the floor of the pony van. She thought about tomorrow. What was going to happen? Was tomorrow the end? She wasn't sure how long she could keep up this constant demand on her legs and back. She tried to count the races she had run in the last two days. Six, she thought, or was it seven. She didn't remember. But she did know that the last one had been the hardest. How fast would the ponies be tomorrow? Would there be a final, championship race? And then would the season end? Would she be free of the dwarf's clutches at least for a while?

From outside of the van, Lightning could hear he sounds of the dwarf tormenting the slave girl, Natasha. She could hear the loud crack of the whip as it struck her body and her long, anguished wails of pain. Apparently her driver was not using a gag. It said enough about this surreal place where she had found herself that someone would not come running at the sound of a girl screaming in pain; that it did not bother the neighbors. Again and again she heard the sound of the whip striking flesh and Natasha's anguished cries. Suddenly, it was done. She heard the sound of her driver and the young girl entering the other side of the pony van, the side meant for human beings, and then, shortly thereafter, the squeals and cries of the poor slavegirl as the dwarf had his way with her.

Often, at night, she could hear the slave girl sobbing in the van through the wall next to her. One morning, when Natasha was about to remove her hood preparatory to her daily shaving, she smiled at the young girl sympathetically. Natasha reacted instantly. She slapped Lightning fiercely across the face, twice, once with each hand. She refilled her mouth with the leather gag. Then she dragged her over to a post which the dwarf used as a whipping post. She affixed Lightning's collar from the back and proceeded to slice at her body with a thin whip. While she was doing it, Lightning tried again and again to beg her to stop, but her voice emerged as inhuman groans. As she was being whipped, Lightning saw the dwarf walking by. He looked up nonchalantly and continued on his way.

In spite of her abuse by her, Lightning still felt sorry for the mousy slave girl. She looked frail, standing only a foot taller than the four foot dwarf. And she looked both older and younger than she probably was. Her small features and tiny stature made her seem like a teenager, but her weary face, the blankness in her eyes, bespoke years of captivity and torment. Lightning guessed that she was about 24 years old. How long could a woman survive such a tormenting life, she wondered.

Lightning fell asleep immediately thereafter. Her body was tired and her mind was tired. She did not dream. But she awoke early, before the slave girl came to retrieve her and, in the darkness of her blinded hood, she prepared herself mentally for the day. Today was the moment of truth, she knew it. Today would probably dictate how she would be treated once she returned to the pony barn, either just another also ran or a pony girl champion. Lightning wanted it so bad that she could taste it.

She went through her normal shaving and feeding as if mesmerized. The bland tasting gruel she was served by the black haired girl did not compare to the sweet porridge she received from her former driver's slave, but today she did not care. She was so lost in herself that she hardly noticed it when, after the black haired girl had put on her racing hood of blue and gold, she was installed in her little cage and the tarp pulled over it, putting her in darkness.

It was not long before she was brought out again. Her flag bedecked sulky cart was waiting for her and the muzzled, black haired slave girl strapped on Lightning's harness and installed her cruel bit. Lightning's driver emerged from the van wearing his shiny, blue and gold racing uniform with the bright yellow wolf on his chest. Lightning saw him stretch and smile. He said something in Russian to her that concluded with the sound of her name, '*Molnya*'. It was unusual to be addressed directly. Something told Lightning that this was no ordinary day.

The dwarf held up two fingers. What did it mean? Was it some good luck sign? She doubted it since her driver did not seem to one of those who relied on luck. Two? What could there be two of? Could he mean two more races? Was that it? Lightning's thoughts were interrupted by the sensation of the dwarf climbing up onto the cart behind her and a tug on the reins that meant to move forward. As they passed the other blue and gold camps, Lightning heard shouts of what she assumed were well wishes from the men there. She even heard some shouted greetings from some of the other camps. Her stomach began to turn as the importance of the day's challenges struck home to her. So many people would be watching. So many people would take an interest in how she did. Lightning trotted through the little copse of woods and entered the little dirt road that led around to the entrance to the track.

Jerzi took her around a couple times at a walking pace. There was a huge crowd and Lightning heard her name called several times. The other pony was jogging through its paces as well, limbering up for the impending duel.

The crowd quieted as the ponies were edged up to the starting line. It wasn't until now that Lightning got a good look at her adversary. She was a tall, lithe, black girl, with skin as black as night. She wore a green and black hood, divided into separate hemispheres as was Lightning's. Her legs were well muscled and she seemed strong and confident. "But she's just a pony like me," Lightning thought to herself. "I can beat her, I have to beat her."

The crowd noise lowered to a near hush as the ready horn sounded. For ten seconds, the two ponies stood poised to leap into action. And then there was the gun. They were off.

It was a nip and tuck race. The black skinned pony was fast indeed. The lead changed four or five times as they scurried around the track. Again, because of her middling overall record during the season, Lightning had the inside track. Jerzi tried desperately to squeeze his cart into the outside, but to no avail. He had to be careful because too much intentional contact between the carts could disqualify him and his pony.

Coming around the home turn, Lightning felt the lash burning into her back. She and the black pony were even. Their legs pumped desperately, each yearning for success and the winner's circle, each dreading the consequences of failure. To the naked eye it seemed that the two ponies crossed the finish at exactly the same time. The yellow ribbon was no help since it draped across the heads of the two ponies equally.

"Photo finish," Burnham said to Jake nervously. "But I think she's got it. Jake had bet his winnings from yesterday on Maddy. In for a penny, in for a pound, he thought. He might as well go all the way. The odds were not as good as yesterday, but they were still better then even. His €25,000 could become €60,000, or zilch.

The two ponies trotted around the track nervously. They knew nothing of photo finishes. They were both perplexed and concerned that no winner had been declared. Lightning felt a huge cavern open in her stomach. Her heart beat heavily as she tried to regain her breath while trotting easily around the track. Just as they pulled up to the grandstand, Lightning heard an announcement over the loudspeaker. She could not understand the language but she knew that it was important since the crowd hushed. Jerzi had her standing perfectly still. After a long, seemingly endless torrent of words, Lightning heard her name, "*Molnya! Molnya! Molnya!*" and Jerzi snapped her reins. Obediently, Lightning took off for a victory lap around the track. "I did it!" she thought to herself wildly. "I did it!"

She felt bad for the black pony who had worked so hard. She knew, once she had pulled into the winner's circle and she saw no trophy, that this was not the last race. For the last race there would be a trophy, of that she was sure. So there must be one more. One more grueling trek around the track. "Okay. Okay" she told herself. "I can do it."

Jake and Burnham watched as the 1500 sulky favorite demolished her rival, finishing three lengths ahead. This did not bode well for Lightning. The pony, Isabella, seemed charged up from her loss yesterday. Jake guessed that she would be looking for vengeance against Maddy. Jake looked at his betting slip. It was worth €65,000 euros. It looked like the odds for the afternoon final would be almost exactly even. €130,000 euros was almost $250,000 dollars. It was a nice piece of change. "Fuck it," he thought. It was money that he had not expected and he didn't want to lose faith in Maddy now, to cause her bad luck by hesitating. He took the ticket back to the cashier, cashed it in and put €65,000 on Lightning's nose.

Four hours later, at about 3 P.M., Lightning and Isabella emerged from the copse of woods that led to the pony encampment. First came Isabella in her red and gold colors. A minute later, Lightning came trotting through. She had had a good rest, had been massaged and teasingly brought close to orgasm. Before they left his camp, Jerzi stood in front of his pony and, smiling, held up a solitary finger.

"One," thought Lightning. "One. This is it."

Lightning did not know that she was racing the pony from the day before. But she knew it as soon as she saw her colors as she warmed up on the track. Yesterday, the other pony had been faster than her. She had won only through the skill of her driver and her last, almost superhuman burst of speed. Slowly, Lightning began to enter a mental zone that she had never experienced before. The noise of the crowd started to fade; her mind seemed to shut down. She could feel the muscles of her legs swell and tighten. She sensed, but did not feel, her driver urge her into place at the starting line. For just one moment, Lightning became conscious of the pony next to her, but then her mind filtered it out. There was nothing but the track ahead and the trigger-like anticipation of the signal gun.

Afterwards, Lightning tried to reconstruct the events of the race. All she could remember was running hard, harder than she ever had before. She remembered the brown dirt of the track ahead, the heavy sounds of her own breath, could remember feeling her heart thumping wildly in her chest.

Jerzi knew that he would have to go wire to wire against Isabella. They would never fall for yesterday's trick again and this was the championship. There was no reason to hold anything back. Isabella was the reigning champ. She would want desperately to repeat. Once the race began, it would all depend on which pony was fastest, today.

The dwarf yelled and screamed imprecations at his pony while snapping his whip on her rump and back. But he knew deep down that this was all show, for the benefit of the crowd and his pony's owner. They would think that he was throwing the race if they saw him doing nothing. He knew that he didn't have to do anything. He sensed that Lightning wanted this. It was all up to her. For either the pony had it in her or she didn't. This was her moment of truth.

Lightning heard none of his yelling and felt no pain from the whip. When she passed the finish line, the yellow tape of the winner draping from her head, she did not even know it. Jerzi had to pull on her reins hard, digging the steel plate from her bit deep into her tongue to get her to slow down and then stop. For a moment, Lightning didn't know what had happened. She saw the sweat glistening body of the other pony pass by at a slow trot. She heard the crowd yelling and screaming. And then she felt a small jerk on her reins, the signal to trot.

She trotted around the track as in a dream. Had she won, she wondered. The other cart pulled over to let her by. She noticed the yellow tape fluttering around her neck. As she realized that she was running the victory lap, her heart nearly burst with joy. She had done it! The crowd was chanting her name as she pulled into the winner's circle. As she had surmised, there was a large trophy there waiting. Someone planted a huge wreath of flowers around her neck. Her owner was there and so was her trainer. She could see the excitement in their faces. Her driver was shaking everyone's hands and someone handed him a large bottle of champagne, almost as large as his arm. He popped open the cork to wild exuberation and chugged some down. Then he came to his pony and stared at her, his grin as wide as his face. With a snap of his fingers, which Lightning could not hear, but she saw the hand motion, the pony fell to her knees. He reached down with one hand and fondled her breasts and kissed them, one by one, sucking hard on her teats until they were hard. Lightning felt the sucking of his lips in her loins. When he was done, he raised his head, smiled at her one more time, and poured a long, cold stream of champagne over her blue hooded head. Everyone around cheered again.

There was a small ceremony where the tournament director presented the trophy to Grobgy. He came up to Lightning and placed a gold disk on her collar. Lightning had seen the disks before on the collars of other ponies, gold, silver or bronze, but hadn't known what they meant. Now she did. From now on, she would be wearing the medallion of a ponygirl champion.

There was only one exception to the rule banning pictures at the tournament, it wouldn't due for all of this to be advertised to the outside world, and that was in the winner's circle after a championship race. Lightning saw that her owner, her trainer and her driver were gathering around her. She saw the man with the camera and realized that she was to be photographed. Somewhere, maybe for a hundred years, there would be a record of her victory. Her picture, with her blue and gold hood and bare breasts, tattooed belly and chest, her naked, hairless sex and black booted feet, would be on somebody's wall with the legend, 'Ponygirl Champion'. And so she stood tall and proud. Today was her day. After the picture, there were handshakes all around.

Jake turned to Burnham in the stands. They had stood and cheered with all of the rest. "How much money are you willing to pay for her," he asked, his lips near Burnham's ear because of the noise. Burnham looked at him and leaned over so that his contract employee could hear him.

"Whatever it takes," he shouted back.

CHAPTER SEVEN
CELEBRATIONS

The party went on all night. Not only had Lightning won the 1500 sulky, but the estate had won the overall championship for the first time. Lightning had put them over the top. Grobgy, a bottle of vodka in his hands, made the rounds through the blue and gold encampment. Lightning didn't know the pony that ran the 3000 meter, but she knew that she did not win when she saw her pass by without a garland, a silver medal hanging from her collar. Later, she could hear the distorted screams and moans of the other pony coming from the neighboring campsite as she was punished brutally for her failure. Her bit made her pleas for mercy sound like some strange, alien tongue.

Her driver had hardly waited for Lightning to be released from his harness before he began fondling her and kissing her breasts. He laid her down on her back on the ground and buried his distorted dwarf's head between her thighs. Maddy was ready, she had earned it and she spread her legs willingly. The dwarf's rough tongue ran the length of her slit up and down while he massaged her thighs. Lightning closed her eyes and sank into a place all of her own. As the hard tongue found its way between her lower lips, her cunt became her world and all else was washed away. Slowly, the small man labored at his task, burying his tongue deep inside her, using it to tickle and rub her hardened clit. A small crowd of well wishers had formed around the couple, but Lightning didn't notice. When Jerzi bit down on her stiff nub of pleasure, she clamped her teeth hard down on her bit, moaning. When he ran the length of his tongue over it repeatedly, lapping at it like a hungry dog, she squirmed and tried to close her legs around her lover's head. Jerzi had his hands on her thighs and kept them splayed to maximize his contact with her sex. The little man drove her to the brink of her crises and then forced a retreat. Lightning groaned and whined, protesting against the delay of her climax. But unlike the times that he had tormented her, exciting her but denying her satisfaction, he returned to his work and raised Lightning to a passionate pitch again.

Lightning's brain began to scream with her need. Her thighs were convulsing, her hips pressing hard against the dwarf's expert mouth and lips. She gave a long, loud scream, audible because of her bit, "Yaaaaaaaaaaaaaaaa! Yaaaaaaaaaaaaaaa!" she cried out. At this, her tormentor allowed her release. Her body shuddered as wave after wave of hard edged pleasure ran through her. She pounded the heels of her black ponygirl boots into the ground and arched her back. The tongue kept her going and, after the first set of almost brutal waves of sensation passed through her, she began another. And then another. She was dazed, in another place, another world, when she felt the Dwarf climb on top of her. Her eyes sprang open inside her hood as she felt his hard rod press into her still trembling sheath. "Ohhhhhhhhhh!" she moaned as she felt herself filled. Jerzi made no effort to work the pony into another paroxysm of pleasure. He didn't need to. Lightning felt that her body was melting around her cunt as he thrust hard into her. She noticed for the first time that they were surrounded by a circle of men who were clapping and chanting her name. "*Molnya! Molnya! Molnya!*" She didn't care. She was being driven to a place of pleasure in her brain where she had never been. "I earned this!" she thought. "I earned this!"

When she felt the dwarf tense and his cock begin to jet his seed into her she came again, slamming her hips into his, grunting and groaning. He groaned too and at his sound of pleasure, the crowd of men cheered.

Jerzi left his pony lying in the dust while he drank shot after shot of vodka with his friends and colleagues. His brother, Giorgi came along and slapped him on the back and hugged him. Lightning was chained to a post for display, as usual after a victory, and she wore her thick garland of flowers around her neck. She was repeatedly manhandled by well wishers and three times she was manipulated to climax. Lightning was still in a stupor when she felt her collar released from the post and a tug on the golden ring in her nose. It was Natasha, the slave girl. The party had moved elsewhere and it was time for Lightning to be fed and put to bed for the night.

The next morning, everything was quickly packed. Hangovers or no hangovers, it was time to break camp and head home. Lightning let the rumble of the road lull her as she tried to put out of her mind what would happen now. Would anything change at the pony barn because of her victory? Would she be treated better? What would her trainer do to her?

It was a six hour drive to Grobgy's estate and they arrived just before dinner. There was a great hubbub of activity around the estate since there would be a big celebration tonight. Lightning and the other ponies were hustled to the barn where they were fed and bathed. They were allowed to rest, tethered in their stalls until the banquet was to begin.

Lightning stood in her stall, her stomach pressed up against the wooden bar that ran across it, her ankles spread wide and affixed to the floor, a leash running from the ring in her nose to the wall that she was facing. A great sense of disappointment washed over her. Here she was where she started. She couldn't remember whether she was in the same stall or not. Was it this the one or one a few stalls over? What difference did it make?

She was wearing her thick, leather gag that filled her mouth and shielded the bottom part of her face. She wanted to scream out in protest, but held back since she knew it would be to no avail. She had to remember for now and forever: she was what she was. She was a ponygirl. For the foreseeable future all she needed to do was to do what she was told. Run when she should run, fuck when she should fuck. Maddy was dead. She was *Molnya*. Everybody said so.

As it began to get dark outside, Lightning heard someone come into her stall behind her. Strong, rough hands ran along her thighs. And between her legs. She welcomed the feel of a thick finger as it insinuated itself between her nether lips. The finger teased her opening until it began to become moist and hot. Lightning's breathing became heavy. She welcomed the distraction of this use of her. She didn't care who it was.

The hand went away and she felt a body dressed in rough work clothes press against hers. Her position at the rail left her slightly bent over forwards and her breasts dangled free from her frame. Two hands encircled them and squeezed them softly. Lightning closed her eyes and moaned. She rubbed her ass against the front of the man and felt his thick, hard cock in his pants. As his fingers pinched and teased her distended nipples, she moaned again.

The hands left and Lightning heard the descent of a zipper. She felt hot hands separate her rear cheeks and a bulbous head presented itself to her rear opening. It had been a while since she had had a good ass fuck. Her trainer, Drabik, had made it almost as sensitive as her pussy and she now welcomed the hard prick, relaxing her muscles as it pushed open the brown ring. It was not as used to penetration as it had been. Jerzi had spilled his seed there a few times, but never drove her to pleasure there. She welcomed the discomfort as the ring was stretched to accommodate her possessor. The hands returned to her heavy, swollen breasts and the cock sank deep into her bowels. For a moment, Lightning had thought that it was her trainer. She had not seen him since the race, but his movements were different, his hands were not the same. It was not him, but whoever it was, Lightning was grateful for her use.

The man dragged his cock across the tissue of Lightning's anal opening causing her to moan with pleasure. He took his time, obviously enjoying the heat of her depths. Lightning felt the familiar tingle in her loins that told her that she was close, and sighed and pressed her buttocks against the strong male body behind her. "Umpf! Umpf! Umpf!" she called as she came, her gag stifling her moans. She felt the man stiffen and heard him grunt and then his cock began to throb and spasm within her. Lightning's body shivered and she groaned deeply as the stiff prick continued to tease her small, round hole.

When the man was done, he withdrew from Lightning's bowels and, after zipping himself up, left without saying a word. Lightning could feel his discharge running down her perineum from her still burning rear portal. Her body felt loose and tingled with the aftermath of pleasure. She was back at the pony barn all right. Just another female to be used as it pleased the many men who worked here. But she had come and that was good. That, and the thrill of the race, was what she would live for.

* * * * * * * * * * *

Burnham and Jake arrived at the Grobgy Estate around 4 P.M. They had taken their time leaving the fairgrounds.

Burnham's tandem pony trailer had been delivered as had Dora and Flora. The dealer's assistant, who had delivered the tall, blond ponies, showed Burnham how to tie them down while Jake fixed breakfast. After the men ate and the slave girls were fed, they got on the road. The slave girls traveled, at Burnham's insistence, in two little built in cages. At least the bottoms were padded, Jake thought.

They had little discussion during the long trip. The only real thing they had to talk about was Maddy and it would have been unwise to do it in front of the slave girls. One could never know.

They stopped at a roadside stand for food and stood outside the camper for a little while so that they could talk.

"We're invited to the Grobgy estate for their celebration," Burnham told Jake.

"You're kidding," Jake replied. "How'd you manage that?"

"I'm a player here, Jake. I've told you that. My pipeline projects are going to bring in a lot of cash. The payroll for the workers will be over $5 million dollars a week. There's going to be three main work camps that will be more like little cities. The day we open the camps there'll be a market for whores, liquor, drugs and places to gamble. People will need food, boots, haircuts, toothpaste, underwear, socks. Got the picture? That $5 million is going to reverberate through the local economy. And that's not to mention what is going to be siphoned off. Everybody wants in, believe me, including Grobgy."

"But that's where Maddy is," Jake said. "You're not going to try and buy her tonight, are you?"

"Let's just say that I will take Grobgy's temperature. I have a lot of goodies to hand out."

"Mr. Burnham," Jake said, "every time you hand out a goody to someone, there's going to be three guys who will think that they should have gotten it. You are going to need a small army to protect you."

"Now you're getting it Jake. That's why I hired Boradin. He'll watch out for the bad guys. And I pay my protection money to the Commission."

"But who will watch Boradin, Mr. Burnham?" Jake asked.

"You will, Jake. You will."

When they arrived, some of Grobgy's grooms took custody of Dora and Flora. They were camped in the visitor's pony camp ground and there was some distance from their camper to the main mansion. He was tempted to take a walk around to see if he could spot Maddy, but he didn't want her to spot him. He didn't want her to get any intimation that there was a rescue attempt going on. He warned Burnham to stay inside and not wander the grounds. "If she sees you, she'll freak out. And then the game is up."

Burnham agreed and they stayed in the visiting team's camp grounds until about seven when the party was to start. Jake took the time to get Klara out of her cage and let her walk around outside with him. He didn't think it appropriate that they wander through the camp, hand in hand like lovers. Klara was a slave girl after all. So he locked her wrists behind her back and installed the shield gag over her face. He ran a leash to the ring in her collar and pulled her gently behind him.

Other fancy trailers had come and there were naked slave girls running to and fro serving drinks and appetizers to fancy dressed men and women sitting in folding chairs outside their vehicles. Occasionally, a ponygirl cart would pass by, the former human females sweating and chugging, the occupants smiling and enjoying themselves.

There was a small brook that ran through the camp site and it emptied into a small pond. The pond was surrounded by white birch trees and wildflowers. A tall oak spread its shade over a large patch of soft grass. The spot was hidden from the campsite by the bright green, late spring foliage. Jake sat down and had Klara kneel down next to him. After removing her leash, he unbound her wrists and unbuckled the gag from behind her head. There was a mild, warm breeze that ran through the little copse where they sat. Jake ran his hand through Klara's flowing blond hair. He thought that he saw the beginning of a smile on her face, some life in her eyes. Suddenly, she moved forwards and placed her hands on his chest, pushing him softly.

"Please, master," she said, and Jake allowed himself to lay back. Klara ran her hands over his chest and began to undo his trousers. She made it clear that she wanted him naked and Jake cooperated by pulling his polo shirt over his head and helping her remove his pants.

When he was naked, Klara laid her body next to his. She caressed his chest again and his stomach and thighs with her hand. Jake could feel her large, soft, white mounds press against him. Her hand fluttered delicately over his hardening sex and then encircled it, grasping it softly.

Klara moved her body atop Jake's and slowly dragged her breasts down his chest and belly, kissing his nipples, running her tongue along his skin. Jake sighed as her mouth kissed the soft flesh of his stomach just above his now hardened member. She then seized his cock with her lips and drew it into her hot mouth.

Jake moaned as he felt Klara's expert tongue dance around the underside of his cock's round helmet. He groaned as she drove his cock deep within her, pressing her lips tightly about the shaft.

Content at having raised her master's passion, Klara released his steel hard rod from her mouth and mounted him, her knees on the grass astride his hips. As she encased his prick in her steaming channel, pleasure flowed through Jake's body. He reached up to caress her breasts and the pretty slave girl presented her twin orbs for his delight. She moaned as he caressed them and began to raise and lower her hips, stroking Jake's swollen member with her warm, tender inner flesh. "Ohhhhhhhhh!" Jake moaned as the hot, moist warmth around his cock washed through him. Slowly, the slave girl raised and lowered herself, reveling in the hot meat that filled her. Jake took her arms and pulled her down. Their lips joined and their impassioned tongues mingled. Jake could feel Klara's hot breasts as they rubbed against him, her nipples hard. He could feel his crises coming. He began to shove his hips up, to meet Klara's strokes. She moaned into his mouth and he could feel her muscles tense.

The slave girl and her master came at the same time. They rocked and pumped at each other's loins while their hands grabbed each other's flesh. Their lips were pressed together fiercely as they moaned their lust and passion to each other. Jake felt the muscles of his slave girl's pussy clamp down on his rod, drawing his essence from him.

The lovers lay quietly in each other's arms for some time. Jake grabbed the sides of Klara's face and planted his lips on hers, kissing her tenderly.

"What has become of me?" Jake wondered as he relished in the post coital rapture. "Have I fallen in love with a slave girl, a woman that I can't really ever have?" For Jake knew that when the job was done, he would have to leave Klara behind. It was a love affair that was doomed. Did she love him? It was a question that could never be answered until she was able to give herself to him freely, not wearing the raiment's of a slave, her tight, black leather collar, the leather bands around her wrists and ankles. But that would never be.

It was the slave girl who first broke their idyllic trance. She slid her body away from his and knelt down in the grass at his feet. When Jake sat up, he saw her kneeling, her knees spread, her hands behind her, her head lowered. The posture of a slave awaiting her master's desires.

It was about six when the couple returned to the camper. Jake had dressed and restored Klara's leash and gag and rebound her wrists behind her. When they arrived, Burnham was on the phone and the pleasingly curvaceous, young brunette slave that he had brought knelt on the floor of the little living area, her forehead to the floor, her breasts crushed atop her thighs, her back arched. Her hands were locked behind her.

Jake showered and changed and at 6:45 he and Burnham walked up to the main house.

The party was a sumptuous affair, better than any of the other parties Jake had been to. The serving slave girls had all been dressed up in Grobgy's racing colors with blue and gold hoods that left their lovely faces uncovered, but which had blue and gold plumes on the top. They all wore heavy, black boots, just like the ponygirls. At a quick glance, they looked like the real thing, but their hands were of course free so that they could serve the guests and they wore the regular slave girl collars.

It amazed Jake that the women who were present, and there were many beautiful ones with daring, stylish outfits, did not take exception to the horde of beautiful, naked slave girls prancing around and turning every man's eye. He wanted to ask one of them but decided against it. Later, he did see some of the couples leading slave girls to the rooms upstairs, rooms available for sexual antics.

Jake and Burnham got separated. He saw him talking to the guy who he decided was Grobgy. They were laughing and joking with one another. Jake had done his homework and he knew that Grobgy was not someone to fuck with. He hoped that Burnham knew what he was doing.

Jake, of course, was packing, but it was his slim Beretta, not the .38 that he carried tonight. It seemed to fit under his sport jacket just a little bit better. He saw a few of the other men were packing heat as well. He was standing alone, nursing his gin when a dark haired fellow came up to him. He had an air of deadly confidence about him. Jake recognized him from a picture he had seen. He was Grobgy's bully boy, Anton Drabik. Even if he hadn't seen his picture, he would have picked him out a mile away. He just looked deadly. And besides, he considered himself to be pretty much a heavy too and it was the nature of gravity to pull heavy bodies together.

Drabik extended his hand to Jake. "Drabik," he said.

Jake took his hand. "Barnes, Jake Barnes," he replied. Nobody was fooling nobody. Drabik was checking him out. Trying to see what he was made of, getting a feel for him. Well he was doing the same thing.

"So, you've come to like our little country, Mr. Barnes?"

"Love it," Jake replied. "But call me Jake."

"Okay, Jake," Drabik acknowledged slowly. "People just call me Drabik."

"You work here?" Jake asked.

"Yes, I do. I'm a pony trainer."

And one of the deadliest ones around, Jake thought. "Interesting," Jake replied. "Did you train any of the winners?"

"As a matter of fact, I did. A couple of them. One of my ponies took the 1500 sulky."

Jake's blood nearly froze in his veins. He prayed to God that he didn't show it. "That so?" he said casually. "Good job. We watched her run. She was terrific."

"Tell me, Mr. Barnes," Drabik asked, swilling what looked like straight vodka in his tumbler, "How did Mr. Burnham get interested in ponygirls?"

"I don't know," Jake replied cautiously. "I never asked. I just do what I'm told, Mr. Drabik. Don't you?"

He could see Drabik tense up. Jake had hit his hot spot right away. Drabik used to command a regiment. Now he worked for a former sergeant in the secret police. There was an icy silence between the two men. It was broken by the appearance of a beautiful black haired young woman dressed in a long, pleated, black gown with small panels covering her breasts that narrowed to straps around her neck. Each breast was perfectly outlined by the delicate fabric. Her nipples pressed outwards like little black darts.

"Anton, where've you been? I want to talk to you," she said in Russian. She gave Jake a lascivious look. "And this is one of the Americans?" she asked in English.

"Yes, Anya," Drabik replied, also in English. "This is Mr. Barnes. He's Mr. Burnham's fetch-it boy."

"Are you a fetch-it boy, Mr. Barnes?" Anya asked, her left hand draped over Drabik's shoulder.

"As a matter of fact, I guess I am," Jake said, sloughing off the insult. "And you?"

"This is Ms. Anya Grobgy, Mr. Barnes. Your host's daughter."

"And are you, Mr. Drabik, Ms. Grobgy's fetch-it boy?" Jake could see Drabik's hand tensed around his glass. Two hits, both bull's-eyes.

Anya laughed. "Please excuse us, Mr. Barnes, I have to talk to Anton about something. Enjoy the party."

Jake knew that Drabik would be trouble. He knew it as soon as he saw the look in his eyes when they first met. He hoped that his attacks covered up his surprise at finding out that he had trained Maddy. He had an idea as to what that entailed and he didn't want to think about it.

Once it got dark outside the pony girl parade was announced. Jake sought out Burnham to make sure that he stayed inside.

"No, I want to see it," Burnham retorted. "She's not going to see me. I'll stay in the back."

The crowd of people, about 200 in all, crowded the porch and front steps of the front of Grobgy's Mansion, the side that faced away from the barns and towards the main road. The long driveway was well lit. The band had come outside and, at a signal, the trumpet let out a flourish. Around the corner of the mansion came the pony girls. They were pulling their racing rigs and were wearing their racing hoods. The band started up some old Stalinist martial tune and the lead carriage, the troika, with blue and gold ribbons fluttering from its sides, a beaming driver encased in his racing duds holding the reins. There was a large circle in front of the mansion and the ponies stretched out along in single file. The ponies were stepping high, their breasts dancing on their chests. As each carriage came by the front of the mansion, which was serving as a kind of reviewing stand, there was a round of applause for the driver and the blue and gold headed, naked ponies. Since during the races some of the ponies doubled up, some of the reserve ponies had been recruited to fill in the gaps. But the crowd didn't seem to care.

Jake saw Maddy pulling her cart, second to last in the long column. Her knees raised high with each step. "She's beautiful," Jake thought. His stomach revolted at the thought of that scumbag Drabik putting his filthy cock in her. Jake saw him, standing next to Grobgy and his daughter, staring intently at Maddy as she went by. Anya noticed it too, and Jake saw a frown cross her face.

* * * * * * * * * * *

Lightning had quailed when she saw her cruel driver again, but he had been all business and, with the help of the little black haired slave girl, Natasha, he suited her up and hitched her to the cart without incident. The carts assembled on the practice track that sat near the barn. The racing track with its fancy grandstand and perfectly maintained track lay out near the pony camp grounds. Once they had all lined up, they waited patiently for someone to signal them to go. Jerzi held Lightning's reins tight, forcing her head back, keeping the steel plate in her mouth tight against her tongue. It was just one more harsh indignity she had to suffer at his hands. Lightning prayed in her mind for the order to move.

Finally, the line of pony carts and carriages began to advance. Persephone and the tall pony who had replaced Lightning were just ahead of her and Lightning was thrilled to have Persephone so near. She wondered when she would ever get to be close to her again. She wanted it badly, even if the two of them were called out to entertain the trainers and grooms some rainy day by kissing and caressing each other on the pony barn floor; she didn't care. She would do anything to get close to the pony that she considered her lover.

When they finally came around the circle and approached the house, Lightning could not really see who was in the crowd. The overhead lights were too bright and her vision too restricted. But she did see who was on the reviewing stand as she approached it. There was her owner, beaming as if he had won the Irish Sweepstakes. Next to him was her trainer, with his dark scowl. On the other side of her owner was the black haired witch who had tormented her just before the racing season began. Lightning tried not to think about what that cruel woman was capable of. She was sure that she had not seen the last of her.

When the last cart had passed, the crowd returned inside for dinner. Lightning and the other racing ponies were returned to their stalls. As a groom fastened her to the wall in front of her and locked in her ankles, Lightning could hear the laughter and banter of the drivers as they got ready to go back to the party. Her driver, the cruel dwarf made no acknowledgement to Lightning when she was unharnessed. As she stood in her stall, awaiting whatever random event was next to happen in her life, she wondered if it meant anything.

* * * * * * * * * * * * * *

Jake left the party relatively early. He didn't want to have another run in with Drabik. Besides, Klara was waiting for him and he had a hunger for her compliant flesh. Burnham left at the same time. He wanted to get an early start in the morning.

"Well?" Jake asked him. "I saw you talking to Grobgy. Anything?"

"He definitely won't sell her," Burnham replied somewhat morosely. "These guys aren't into ponygirl racing for the money. Just the opposite. He's determined to keep her."

"Do you want to consider other alternatives?" Jake asked, knowing the answer.

"No, Jake, for the last time. No special ops stuff. I told you."

"Just asking, Mr. Burnham," Jake said defensively. "It's my job."

"I know, I know," Burnham acknowledged.

"I do have another idea," Jake said. "Grobgy's definitely a gambling man. If we had a pony that could race against Maddy and beat her, maybe we could get him to put her up in a stakes race."

"That's a good thought," Bertram replied. "He wants one of the big supply contracts from me. It's worth about three million. I could put that up against Maddy. Now that I think he'll go for."

"The only problem is where would we get a pony like that? She's already beat the best in the country." Jake said anxiously.

"We'd have to get one outside the country. Train her ourselves. Someone who could beat Maddy."

"But that would take months!" Jake exclaimed.

"Undoubtedly," Burnham answered. "But do you have a better idea?"

Jake admitted that he did not. It took two months to train Maddy and by the end of the fourth month she was a star. She had natural talent for the sport, as much as Jake hated to admit it. They would need time to recruit someone. That could take a month. By the time they were ready, it would be racing season again. And Grobgy wouldn't gamble with one of his prize ponies during racing season. That meant that the stakes race couldn't take place until the middle of October, five months from now. Maddy would have to stay a ponygirl for all that time.

* * * * * * * * * * * * * * * * *

It was pitch dark when Lightning was called out of her stall. It had begun to rain outside and she could hear the rolling blasts of the angry night skies and see the flashes of the electrical charges through the skylights in the barn. It was one of the old caretakers who brought her out. She followed him on her leash through the warren of stalls and into the common area. There were three people standing there. She recognized them all although the light was dim. In the center stood her owner, the tall, heavy set, black haired man with the thick handlebar moustache, who had claimed her on her first day by fucking her on a hay bale in front of his laughing and cheering workers. On his right stood her trainer, the man who had broke her to a leash, who had trained her to run, who had made her a sexually subservient beast. On the left was the terribly cruel dwarf who had tormented and abused her the past few weeks but who had also driven her to victory, who had finally and permanently made her into a ponygirl. They were sharing a bottle of vodka, laughing and joking with each other.

"Well, you were right," Grobgy said to his henchman, Drabik. "She is special. Probably the best ponygirl we've ever had."

"I'll drink to that," Jerzi said as he took the liter sized bottle of clear white firewater from his soon to be former employer's hand. He took a large gulp. "She's a great fuck, too," he told the others. It was something that Drabik knew well. But Grobgy had only a limited experience with her. She was standing no more than three feet from the men and he examined her breasts and belly with the eye of an expert.

"It's a long summer. I'll have to get better acquainted with my star ponygirl."

Drabik reached over and retrieved the bottle from the cruel visaged dwarf. He took a pull. "She likes it in the ass," he said. "And she has a very skilled mouth."

Lightning could not understand the strange language that the men spoke, but she had no doubt that the men were talking about her. Her stomach churned at the thought that they had come here to beat her. The old man had unleashed her and she stood nervously before the men awaiting an order. She shuffled her feet and her firm, pleasant breasts swayed. Her nipples were hard with fear and something else. These men were going to use her. Of all the ponies in the barn, of all the ponies who had raced and won, they wanted her. Her pussy began to burn with expectation.

Drabik moved first. Slowly, he walked around her, his heavy boots treading ominously on the wooden floor. Lightning knew that she dare not move, not if she wished to avoid a whipping. These men were harsh taskmasters and would brook no disobedience. When Drabik got behind her, he pushed Lightning's torso so that she was bent over at a 45 degree angle. He used his boots to kick her feet apart. Stepping up against her, he took her breasts in his hands and presented them to his companions. They smiled when Lightning sighed at the hot hands on her breasts.

"I told you so," Drabik stated to his boss, his voice a little slurred. He was drunk.

"Remember when I did this?" he asked, running his hand between Lightning's thighs from behind and seizing her sex. When Lightning was just a new pony, on her first day of training, Drabik had forced her to orgasm before her owner and his daughter by stroking her pussy from behind, just as he was doing now. At the time, Lightning was mortified to be so callously used in front of her owner and the strikingly handsome young woman. But now, Lightning's cunt was already wet and Drabik was able to slide his fingers the length of her slit. He laughed and said something to the other men that Lightning didn't understand but made them laugh too. Drabik's hand began to tease Lightning's engorging nether lips, stroking them, squeezing them. He pressed a finger against the bud at the top of Lightning's sex and she moaned with desire.

"Give her your cock, Anton," Grobgy called out to the assassin. "She wants it."

Drabik's cock was as hard as steel. He had yearned to possess Lightning's flesh for too long. He zipped open his fly and freed his hard pole. Bending his knees he was able to slip its head along the length of Lightning's sheath. She shuddered in response, knowing that she would soon be impaled on it. She looked at the men in front of her and saw the raw lust in their eyes. Her breasts dangled invitingly before them as they echoed her body's motion, trembling and shivering. Drabik pushed his prick against the gate to the ponygirl's hot canal and eased himself in. "Mmmmmmmmmmmmm!" she moaned through her gag as the sensation of being filled overwhelmed her. If the men could have seen her eyes they would have seen them rolling back as passion overtook her. Deliberately, Drabik sawed his tool back and forth in Lightning's moist, hot tunnel. She started to falter, her knees going weak, her mind beclouded. Drabik grabbed the ring at the back of her collar with his strong right hand and held her up, freezing her in her half bow before the other men. He started to pound his meat into her with determination and her breasts jerked and bobbed and swung against each other like they had a life of their own.

Lightning was being driven to the heights of passion by the insistent cock. Her nipples burned with desire and her stomach tensed. Weeks ago, she would have been humiliated to display her naked passion to these callous, lustful men. But now she relished the desire she inspired in them. She wanted them to want her and the knowledge that they stood there, their eyes burning into her body, waiting their turn with her, drove her wild with lust. When she came, she groaned loudly. She called out "Eh! Eh! Eh! Eh!" each exclamation matched by a mind wrenching contraction of her pussy's walls.

Drabik felt her squeezing his pulsing meat and he came, pumping his hot fluid inside her. Lightning felt it awash within her and her contractions, which had begun to fade, started anew. "Ohhhhhhhhhhhhh!' she moaned as Drabik grunted his pleasure behind her, pounding his thighs against her rear. "Ohhhhhhhhhh!" she cried again. She would have fallen had Drabik not taken hold of her collar and even as he withdrew his cum covered cock from her crevasse, Lightning began to swoon.

"Good work, Anton, but I think you've put her to sleep on us," Grobgy joked.

"I can wake her up," Jerzi responded. He stepped forward and grabbed Lightning by the ring in her nose. The ring peeked out from a hole in the ponygirl's hood designed to keep free her nostrils. Lightning was woken from the reverie that Drabik's cock had induced in her. There was a stanchion in the middle of the room about three feet wide and about three feet high. Jerzi dragged the ponygirl to it and pushed her torso forwards over the top. There was a strap in the middle of the bottom on the other side and Jerzi tied Lightning's nose ring tightly to it. He went behind her and strapped her thighs together just above the knees and at her ankles and fastened them to the stanchion.

"Her legs are the only place I haven't really whipped her," Jerzi told the others. "I want her to remember me well when I come back in August."

The dwarf took another long drink of vodka and handed the bottle over to his companions. He stepped up on a bench and drew a four foot long rattan cane from the wall.

Lightning heard the whip swish through the air behind her. She knew that pain was coming and tried to steel herself against it. She hated being whipped and would never get used to it. She knew that shortly she would be screaming and begging and pleading to no avail. She just hoped that it would be short.

The dwarf landed the first blow just below the rounded edges of Lightning's rear, just at the top of her rear thighs. Her body jerked as it registered the pain and in spite of herself, as she knew she would, Lightning cried out in pain. The next blow landed a inch or two lower, making a loud 'cracking' sound that echoed through the barn. Lightning squealed with the pain and frantically tried to pull her legs apart so that she could at least try to evade the blows. But she was strapped down tight and her efforts just produced a wrenching pain in her nose.

Except for the laughter of the men, the sound of a whip striking skin and Lightning's piteous moans, muffled as they were by her thick, mouth filling gag, there was silence in the barn. It was filled with more than thirty other female souls, all former women. But none of them dared to make so much as a whine of fear. All of the ponygirls knew what was happening. One of them was being whipped. Which one they did not know, but they were all glad that it wasn't them. They cowered silently in their stalls praying that they would not be next. Soon, the grooms would come and put them to bed. If they could survive the rest of the day without pain and violence being inflicted upon them they would be happy. Tomorrow was tomorrow and who knew what would happen then. But ponygirls did not think about tomorrow. They tried not to think about yesterday. For them, there was only the here and now.

Jerzi moved his strokes down Lightning's thighs with mathematical precision. He struck the blows with such force that it lifted him off of the floor. Lightning was crying and blubbering, her pleas for mercy emerging as howls and groans. Her thighs were aflame with pain. They glowed red from the bottoms of her pale white rear globes to just above the straps that held her knees closely together. Jerzi paused, and Lightning prayed that he was done. But he had stopped only to fortify himself with another swig of the 120 proof vodka. He let the fire burn his throat and handed the bottle back to Grobgy. The gangster and his minion stood in mute appreciation of the dwarf's skills with the whip. Lightning's moans and cries made Drabik hard again. Grobgy was rubbing his long, fat cock unconsciously through his pants as he watched.

After his pause, Jerzi began again. His target this time was the hard flesh behind Lightning's shins. For his weapon, he had chosen a 1 ½ inch round solid oak dowel. It had a leather handle and was finely polished. It was about two feet long, almost as long as Jerzi's arms. Jerzi reared back and drove the club down hard against the tight muscles on the back of Lightning's shins. She had not anticipated this and the excruciating pain made her nauseous even as she moaned deeply. Bile rose into her throat as the second blow landed, just below the first. Jerzi's height made what would have been a difficult angle for someone taller a natural for him. Five times he struck the defenseless muscles; five times Lightning body wrenched with agony.

The cruel, scar faced dwarf tossed the club aside after the fifth blow. He pulled a bench over to the stanchion, behind Lightning's legs, and he jumped up on it. It was just the right height for him. He drew his rod from his trousers and began to run its bulbous head along the joinder of Lightning's rear globes. Lightning was still moaning and crying, but she could feel the conscienceless cock drag along the valley between her cheeks. The dwarf bent his knees and teased Lightning's sticky, wet slit with it, lubricating himself with the remnants of Lightning's and Drabik's mingled discharges. He encircled his cock with his gnarled right hand and began to stroke it. His eyes closed to slits as he forced himself to the edge of orgasm. Even through her soul wrenching dismay and the remnants of her excruciating ordeal, Lightning knew what he was doing. She was to be the receptacle of his lust, a depository for his passion. She would meet this evil man again. Lightning knew it. Fear tore through her at the thought.

When Jerzi was ready, his cock ready to explode, he leaned over and pushed its fat head through the compressed flower of Lightning's behind. The tearing flesh burned her and she groaned as he plunged his cock deep within her bowels. She felt him pump once, twice and a third time and then heard the telltale groan of his climax. His hands gripped her hips tightly as he drew his weapon of flesh back and forth across Lightning's pained anal ring. When he was done, his last jet of cum splashed inside her, he withdrew his cock, slapped her hard on the ass, and then hopped off of his mount. He stuffed his brown stained cock back into his pants. "I'll get one of your bitches to clean that off later," he said to Grobgy. "Now it's your turn."

Grobgy motioned the other men to release Lightning from her perch. She felt herself pulled to her feet and hustled over to be presented to her lord and master. The two men released the ponygirl and she stood fearfully before her owner. Tomorrow, she knew, she would not be able to walk. The damage to her leg muscles had not fully set in yet although they throbbed and ached. Grobgy reached his hands out and grabbed the sides of Lightning's face. There was silence in the barn and Lightning could hear the pelting rain outside and the rolling thunder overhead. Grobgy peered deeply into Lightning's eyes. Her body trembled at the cruel, hard eyes that she saw. He held her there for several moments, moments that seemed to Lightning to be filled with his ominous power over her.

The gangster, ponygirl king, killer, slid his hands behind Lightning's head and loosened her gag. He pulled it out and tossed it aside. He stepped back and, placing his hands on the ponygirl's shoulders, pressed her to her knees. His hands drew out his sword of flesh; it was already rigid. Lightning knew her task.

Due to the angle of her collar, Lightning had to tilt her head downwards in order to seize Grobgy's hot, reddish cock with her lips. She raised herself on her knees and enveloped it, dragging her tightened, broad lips down its shaft. She worked the knob with her tongue and then drew her head back so that her lips once again scraped its length. Here was her power. She could make this man groan and sigh with pleasure. Once she had laid claim to his cock with her mouth, she knew that he would seek out its moist heat again and again. She pushed her head down again and, laying her tongue flat underneath it, used it to tease its underbelly as she drew her head back again.

Grobgy moaned deeply. His lust was on the boil from what he had witnessed and he was ready to pour his soul out through his cock. When Lightning went down again, his cock began to jerk and pulse. She could feel his hot fluid strike the back of her mouth as his cum jetted out from his tool. His hands grabbed her blue hooded head and squeezed it, pushing it down hard on his loins. Lightning felt Grobgy's cock slip into her throat. She coughed slightly but then clamped her lips and mouth down hard on the throbbing rod. The moment seemed suspended in time. Grobgy, his knees bent, his back arched, his hooded eyes looking skywards, let the constrictive heat of Lightning's throat and mouth flow through him. It was a dramatic tableau and a long, snaking line of lightning struck outside, silhouetting the engaged pair in the light that flashed through the broad, open barn doors.

Grobgy eased his still tingling cock from Lightning's mouth. He patted her on the head and reached for the bottle of vodka. He staggered backwards slightly as he tipped his head back to take a long swig. His pony girl knelt before him, her knees spread, her arms locked behind her back. Her round, heavy breasts curved up invitingly.

He could see the mark that had been burned into her belly, the fierce, yellow wolf, his prideful symbol. Her blue encased head, tilted upwards by her collar deprived her of all humanity. She had no face and never would again. But she was a beautiful, passionate animal. Yes, he would visit the pony barn often this summer. She was his as much as any stone or tree or blade of grass on his vast estate and he would use her as he would anything that could bring him pleasure.

Lightning heard the men laugh. They were finished with her, she knew. One by one they stroked her head as they passed her by on the way out of the barn. Before he left, her trainer recovered her gag from the barn floor and reinstalled it in her mouth.

The old man was sitting on a stool by the entrance. He had watched the whole thing. He pitied these poor ponygirls. They were good to look at and fun to watch, and that was all he could do at his age was watch. But they suffered terrible abuse, worse than any horse or dog. What other animal would be beaten so severely just for the pure joy of it?

He got up from his stool and leaned over, stroking the pony's long, brown tail behind her anonymous head. He murmured soothing words to her and jingled the gold medal that hung from her collar. The ponygirl looked up at him, grateful for some tenderness and the reminder of her achievement. They could do what they wanted to her, but she knew that soon, she didn't know exactly when, they would be cheering her on again, intent on her victories.

The old man reattached the leash to her collar and gently pulled her to her feet. He was still cooing to her. "Poor little *Molnya*," he said to her soothingly in Russian. "Pretty, little *Molnya*."

Another snake of light crawled across the sky outside the barn illuminating the young female and the old man.

He knew that they kept the ponygirls ignorant, but he wanted her to know. She deserved to know now that she was a champion. He pulled her to the doorway and waited. A long, crooked line of light dashed across the sky. He pointed to it eagerly and then to the Cyrillic writing on the former woman's chest. "*Molnya! Molnya!*" he said to the hooded and bound pony urgently, needing her to understand.

The ponygirl cast her eyes up to the rain filled sky. "Lightning! My name is Lightning!" she yelled out in her mind. "My name is Lightning!"

She looked at the old man. There was another bolt of crooked light above them and then a large crash. "*Molnya!*" the man said, nodding and pointing to the light. "*Molnya!*"

End Book Three